DEATH LOG

The Fifth Anna Harris Novel

A V IAIN

Chapter One

WHEN I GET OFF the phone to fellow friend—and assassin—AA, it's around midnight.

We're going to meet in about fifteen minutes.

The Roughed Diamond: a bar in Shepherd's Bush.

I stand alone in my kitchen, feeling the gentle chill of the winter draughts all around me.

I've been trying as hard as possible to save money. Ever since Brian Mathewson dropped me from his assassins' roster—dropped *all* his assassins, for that matter—I've had to instil a fresh wave of thriftiness about my person.

Although, in all likelihood, I have more than enough saved in the bank—more than I'll *ever* be able to spend—I can't help but feel a little hypnotised watching my balance diminish a little more each day.

What if it *does* reach zero?

What then?

Perhaps I'll have to open shop as a cleaner, or a rubbish collector, probably the only jobs that I'd 'officially' qualify for.

I glance down at the now-empty cup of tea on the kitchen counter, the simple memory of the sweet hot liquid once within already sending warm, throbbing, comforting waves through my blood.

When I breathe in now, the pain's almost gone. My ribs have had a chance to heal . . . one of the good aspects of not having to go through with any hits; it's allowed my body a brief pause to recuperate. And my calf muscle which got shot through in my final 'job' feels in decent shape too.

Nothing that six hours of surgery couldn't fix.

Outside, beyond the drawn curtains, I can hear the gentle *pitter-patter* of drizzle falling against the kitchen window. If I breathe in deeply, I can just about make out that clean, damp scent of the rain too.

I roll my arms back in their sockets, hoping to ease a little of the tension out of my shoulders. I shouldn't *have* any reason to feel tense. Brian cast me out. Absolved me of ever becoming involved with him again.

Yeah, except that's not quite the case.

In fact, Brian Mathewson is the driving reason for my meeting with AA in fifteen minutes' time.

If only I could get shot of Brian for good . . .

As I stand, half leaning my weight up against the kitchen counter, my tortoiseshell cat—*Lizzie*—appears in the kitchen doorway. With a diminutive *brurr* . . . a sound something between a *purr* and a miaow . . . she pads over to me, rolls her warm, fuzzy body up against the legs of my tracksuit bottoms.

I crouch down and then lift her up in my arms, bring her up against the V-neck t-shirt I'm wearing. Lizzie closes her eyes as she purrs away to herself, her paws all gone slack, her tail dangling down in mid-air.

I think long and hard about the meeting with AA.

I could cancel it easily.

I could just pick up the phone, tell him that we can choose another night for this *impromptu* meeting.

Yeah . . . and a seventy-year-old man in a clown suit might just rap on my door and demand a cup of sugar.

If AA's anything at all, it's *inflexible*. When he states a date, let alone a *time*, then you're expected to stick to it religiously.

Or prepare to face the consequences.

And, as one myself, I well know the perils of getting on the wrong side of an assassin.

Realising that there's nothing else for me to do, aside from meet with AA, I gently let Lizzie down, allow her to descend to the floor.

Then I set about making myself presentable.

Chapter Two

THE TAXI DROPS ME OFF on the street corner of The Roughed Diamond.

Feeling in a good mood—*Thrifty Anna be damned*—I give the driver a nice tip.

It's almost Christmas, after all.

The driver thanks me with an almost antiquated gesture, tipping the rim of his baseball cap and wishing me a good evening before I let myself out into the freezing drizzle.

The Roughed Diamond features violet lighting, which spills out onto the street. The window which looks out at me has matching curtains, and I can't help thinking that—for a bar—the whole façade of the place is immaculately well kept.

As I tread on past the bouncer—a rotund man dressed in a tuxedo, a silver earring dangling from his left ear, with only wispy grey hair saving him from outright baldness—I'm fairly certain that I can smell a minty odour on the air.

That's probably as good a clue as any to what sort of place this is.

AA's type of place.

A gay bar.

Once I pass through—yet another—violet curtain, and into the bar area proper, I feel a little less self-conscious about having gone with a fake mink fur coat for this evening.

I look over the drinkers, the ones slouched up at the walnut counter of the bar: mostly well-dressed men, still in their work suits; it being Friday I don't suppose there's been much of an opportunity to get changed.

A pair of women sit at the other end of the bar, each of them in a sequined dress, their heads bowed low over their colourful— apparently *fruity*—cocktails.

I can't help but feel that the two of them are staring long and hard at the space between my shoulder blades as I make my way across the exposed wooden floorboards of the bar, and into the gloomier section of the place.

Where AA agreed we should meet.

Techno music—at least I *think* that's what it is—drawls out through unseen speakers, and I'm glad that it's kept down to a tastefully low volume. And even as I catch myself thinking that thought, I realise that I'm becoming my mother . . . and, in my mid-thirties, that's really quite damning.

The air is kept comfortably warm, so that the icy air from outside, which nibbled away at my cheeks, becomes a distant memory. I feel a pleasant, shuddering wave pass over the surface of my skin as if my body thanks me for bringing it in from the cold.

It takes my eyes a couple of seconds to adjust to the dim lighting in the further reaches of the bar, and another few seconds still to identify AA, sitting at a round table, drumming his fingers, impatiently, against the immaculately lacquered surface.

AA wears a neatly cut black suit. The satin lapels give off a slight sheen in the violet lighting. In a way, the sheen of the lapels compliments his slicked-back, well-gelled hair.

Before AA, on the table, he has either a gin and tonic or a glass of water with a slice of lime in it. As I approach him, I get a strong whiff of sandalwood. It's almost overpowering as I shrug off my fake fur jacket and hang it over the back of the chair opposite, revealing the simple, black cocktail dress I wear underneath.

AA continues to stare down into his glass for another few seconds before deigning to raise his glance to me. His eyes look troubled, there're deep, dark rings about the bases of his sockets. He looks like a man who's spent a good long while Thinking Things Over.

Hence this impromptu meeting, I suppose.

"Evening," he says, reaching for his drink, bringing it to his lips and then taking a sip.

"Actually," I say, looking around us, and seeing that the other tables are deserted, "it's morning now."

AA meets my eye for a second, making an 'oh' shape with his lips before returning to focus on his drink. "What're you drinking?" he says.

Only then do I realise that there's a stick-thin woman—a *girl* really—in a pair of skinny jeans and a clean, crisp, white vest, standing over our table. She has her thumbs tucked into the back pockets of her jeans, and looks on the verge of yawning at any second as she awaits my order.

"A fizzy water?" I say.

The girl hovers there for a few seconds, as if she's unable to quite believe my order—*at several minutes past midnight*—but she finally relinquishes.

But not before AA gets in a freshener on his own drink.

It turns out that he *is* drinking gin and tonic.

Once the girl has gone to fetch our order, a silence engulfs the table.

AA reaches for his drink, knocks the rest of it back, wincing a touch at the—*apparently*—bitter taste. When he replaces the emptied glass on the table top, he mumbles so quietly that I almost miss his words. "Did you bring it?" I just about muster from his grumbling tone.

Of course I know what he means by 'it'. I dig about in the inside pocket of my fur coat. I produce the memory stick from within, watch on as AA's eyes wander back and forth in their sockets. "I'm not going to leave it lying around at home, am I? Of course I brought it along—I bring it along everywhere I go."

What I don't add, because the two of us know it implicitly, is that the memory stick in my possession could—*very well*—bring the entire United Kingdom to its knees. It could, not to get *too* melodramatic about it, bring about a nationwide revolution.

My little Death Log.

AA gives an almost undiscernible nod, then reaches for his empty glass, apparently not having realised that it's empty.

I slip the memory stick back into my inside pocket and decide that this is my chance. "What's this about, AA?" I say.

AA continues to stare at his empty glass, and I can't help thinking that he's stooped in some sort of depression, though what he has to be depressed about is somewhat beyond me. AA —*unlike me*—has been living a pretty hedonistic lifestyle.

If anything, he should be up where the clouds float around.

"You think," he says, still staring at his glass. "You think, Anna . . ."

"What?" I say. "What'd you think?"

He looks up at me.

Meets my eye.

"You think you could lend me some money?"

Chapter Three

THE WAITRESS RETURNS with our orders—my fizzy water and AA's gin and tonic.

I also notice that she lays a folded-up receipt down in a ceramic saucer, something which, most likely, in a past life, was an ashtray.

If AA notices the receipt then he shows no sign of it.

I busy myself with my fizzy water, turning my attention to the bubbles rising up to the surface and popping. When I take a sip, I realise that it has a faint lemon zest to it. I suppose that a bar like this has to add something—*anything*—to even the simplest of items to justify the cost.

Gourmet water, there's nothing like it.

I absorb what AA's said, turn his words around in my mind, study them from all angles. "I thought you were flush," I say.

AA doesn't give any answer beyond a faint grumble at the back of his throat. He stares at his newly delivered gin and tonic, apparently considering its deeper implications before he'll take a sip.

"You're telling me that you spent it all?" I say. "That you spent everything you saved up working for Brian?"

Again, another one of those grumbles at the back of the throat.

"Christ, AA," I say in reply, losing myself in the bubbles of my fizzy water in the same way AA loses himself in the stillness of his gin and tonic.

Another pregnant silence looms large over the table, and I glance around, hoping that there might be some sort of *other* diversion to sweep me away from this marauding moroseness.

But, no.

Here, in this part of the bar, me and AA are all alone.

"How much?" I say, glancing up at AA.

He mumbles a six-figure number.

"Fuck off!" I blurt out, unable to hold myself back.

I compose myself, tell myself to calm down.

I fix AA with a glance across the table, do my best to meet his eye, although he's doing *his* best to avoid mine. "Are you serious?" I say. "You really need that much?"

". . . Yeah," is the sound which finally escapes AA's lips.

I breathe in deeply and then sigh it out.

I glance around this little, gloomy part of the bar.

In the near distance, I can hear the sound of stool legs scraping against wooden floor. Babbling conversations of drinkers preparing to leave.

Although this isn't the type of place where the barman will bellow out 'Last orders!', I can tell by the receipt on my and AA's table that 'last orders' have come and gone.

That it's high time for us to pay up and leave.

I look back to AA. "Christ," I say again, "how'd you spend it all?"

A faint smirk pulls at the corner of AA's lips. He gives a slight shake of his head, apparently enjoying a private joke with himself, or perhaps revisiting some great, raging excess. When he looks back up at me, his expression is stone again. "Please, Anna, there's no one else I can turn to."

I meet his eye for a long while and then I puff out my cheeks.

Although there's no doubt I can afford the money AA's asking from me, there's also no doubt that it'll make a dent in my finances. And a pretty sizeable one at that.

I can hardly believe that I've made my mind up as I get out a firm, apparently unshakable, "Okay."

AA brightens a touch at this. Gives me the flash of an authentic smile this time—instead of a smirk. "Thanks, Anna," he says, and I notice that he's slurring his words a little.

When I glance back over my shoulder, I see that the waitress is peeping into our area of the bar. I catch her eye and she gives me a cool stare, her gaze never quite reaching my eyes, but floating up and over my scalp. "We're closing," she says, clean and matter of fact.

She disappears back behind the bar as quickly as she came.

I can hear the *clink* and *tinkle* of glasses being collected; can smell the chemical stench of disinfectant being sprayed across tables; the *zip* of cloth moving over surfaces, wiping them down.

I glance to AA, then look to the receipt. "Do you want me to get this?" I say.

AA gives me a smile in return, then a shake of his head. "Please, Anna," he says, "I invited *you*."

Next, he reaches for the ceramic saucer, unfolds the receipt then reaches inside his jacket pocket. He lays out several twenty-pound notes. I don't see how many, exactly, but I can tell that it's a decent wad.

He finds his feet somewhat clumsily, a couple of times slipping on the—to my knowledge—extremely dry and firmly grounded floor, before managing to find his balance. He gives me another one of those drunken smiles, his rosy cheeks reminding me of some sort of merry drunkard: a look which makes me glad that I never met *that* sort of man . . . to think that I could be dealing with that every night at home . . .

"Anna," AA says, coming up to me, and then, quite unexpectedly, winding his fingers about mine. "There was one *other* thing."

"What?" I say, already feeling a dawning sense of dread for asking.

"You see, there's a prob . . . a prob . . ."

" 'A problem' ?" I put in, trying to help him out.

Now that he's got the Big Ask out of the way, it seems that he can afford to let down a little of the sober act he's been putting on.

AA extends the index finger of the hand not currently holding mine. He waggles said finger directly at the tip of my nose. "Yes!" he says, far too loudly—loudly enough so that the waitress sends a searing glare in our direction from her position behind the bar.

"Shh," I say, wriggling my fingers free from his hold.

AA sways from side to side like a sapling in a thunderstorm.

I reach out and grab hold of his shoulder, stopping him from toppling over. "What?" I say. "What's the *problem?*"

AA presses his lips so tightly together that the blood drains from them. He looks back at me not a little solemnly. "I'll tell you in the car."

Chapter Four

AA HAS PARKED his car around the back of the bar, down a side alley. Just from looking over AA's car, I can begin to see where the money has gone, why he's in such 'urgent' need of a loan.

Although I know very little about cars, I can tell that this one —from its sleek, rounded curves; its lack of back seats; its ample bonnet—is an expensive model. A sports car, I suppose. It has a canary-yellow paintjob which either seems extremely well kept because of the constantly falling drizzle or because AA has it buffed up daily.

As I look the car over, I see that it's parked on double-yellow lines.

When AA squeezes the zapper, makes the car's hazard lights blink intermittently and give a pair of merry toots on its horn, I note the plastic-wrapped notice taped to his windscreen.

Danger-red.

A parking fine.

I say nothing about it and AA doesn't seem to see it at all.

He turns his attention to the driver's door.

To attempting to find where he slips his key into the lock.

As I stand back, just watching, feeling the drizzle dampen my fur coat, the sight puts me in mind of an orangutan who's just come across a car in the middle of his enclosure, and that he's attempting to figure it out.

In the end, though, mostly in the hope of not contracting pneumonia, I decide to help him out. "I think it's already unlocked," I say. "I think that's what you did with the zapping."

AA glances up at me, a touch perplexed for a moment, and then a drunken grin appears. He gives a shake of his head, as if he's just as puzzled at his own behaviour as I am, and then —*finally*—he opens up the driver's door.

The passenger door—*my door*—soon pops open too.

I clamber inside.

Once AA has brought the driver's door shut with a too-loud *thud*, I breathe in that thick, strong scent of new-car smell. And since I'm sure AA's car is a good few months old, I'll bet that part of his cleaning service—the same one which keeps the paintwork buffed to a shine—accounts for keeping the car smelling *new*.

For the longest time, AA seems a touch perplexed by the controls. He slips me a sidelong glance as if *I'm* going to be able to help him out.

I'm not about to offer to drive for him.

For one thing, I'm not on the insurance for the car, and since I've just agreed to loan AA a significant amount of money—what I once might've considered to be something approaching a *fortune* —I'm not about to risk losing more, or getting sent to prison, just because AA can't take his drink.

It's only five minutes from the bar back to my house, but, all the same, I know that I should ask the question.

"Are you okay to drive?" I say, thinking about all those gin and tonics. "We can take a taxi if you want."

AA holds a hand up to me as if he was some sort of medieval king silencing the fool in his court. He slips the plastic fob into a slot and—*apparently on a roll*—stabs the clearly marked ON-OFF button.

The engine roars to life . . . and that's no exaggeration, it really *does* roar.

Leaving it in Neutral, AA revs the engine several times, and I watch on as his smile widens more and more as he savours the sound.

I feel the vibrations passing up through my seat, sending a thrill through my stomach.

A chilly sensation creeps up my spine and I can't help thinking that this is a Very Bad Idea Indeed . . . that I could ask AA to let me out if I—

AA releases the handbrake and switches the car out of Neutral. The car lurches forwards and down, off the curb AA had parked it on. He trundles us out to the opening of the side alley and, with an extremely exaggerated glance from side to side, pulls out into the main road.

Thankfully—at this time—the streets are pretty much clear of traffic.

Only the odd lonely drunken reveller making their sad way towards the taxi rank on the corner; their hunched, huddled-up postures made all the more miserable by the unending drizzle.

AA opens up the throttle as we plough along the street, keeping the steering surprisingly steady. I'm fairly certain that

AA's skill of driving while drunk is one which he has perfected after years—*decades?*—of practice.

Unlike most drunk drivers, AA sticks strictly to the speed limit, and he is theatrically meticulous with his signalling and looking.

Still, it doesn't make it any more comfortable to be his passenger.

I decide to use humour to take my mind off things.

"Were you a driving instructor in a previous life?" I say.

In profile, AA gives me another of his grins, and drives onwards.

Up ahead, I see a police car waiting to pull out from a side road. A pair of policemen sitting in the front seats, their fluorescent yellow-and-blue jackets making them seem odd—out of place—within their car.

My heart does a tiny leap, and I look to AA.

But he's not paying attention to me.

As we pass by the policemen waiting to pull out, AA gives them both a mock salute and a smile, then drives on past.

My pulse now pounding in my throat when I turn to glance over my shoulder, and out through the rear window, I watch the police car slip out of the side alley and drive off in the opposite direction, on the other side of the road.

I allow myself to breathe again.

"So," I say, now feeling a little more confident that the road ahead has opened up—and that there're no other cars in sight. "What was this *other* thing?"

AA grips the steering wheel tightly, so tightly, in fact, that I see that his knuckles have turned white while he does so. His gaze, though, remains fixed on the road ahead—again as if he was taking his driving test. He swallows hard, making his Adam's apple bob in his throat. He flips me a side-on glance, then says, "It's a biggie, Anna."

"Really?" I say, flashing my eyebrows, then looking out to the road ahead. "Bigger than the better part of a million pounds?"

"If it's a problem, you can feel free to say no, okay?"

I glance at AA, see that there's no joviality remaining in his expression. That he's now one-hundred-percent focussed on his driving. On keeping the car straight in the road. "You don't want me to get back involved with Brian Mathewson, do you?"

AA gives a slight smile, then shakes his head. "No," he says, "nothing like that."

I allow the tension to leave my muscles.

Me and AA have a deal with Brian, a sort of truce.

I have the dirt on him—in the form of the memory stick; the Death Log—and he has the dirt on us, in terms of his wide-ranging connections.

If he wanted us dead—*truly* wanted us dead—he could make it happen with very little effort.

"Anna," he says. "I was—"

Seeing where we are, I cut him off. "This is the turning, just here," I say.

Despite my swiftly delivered instructions, AA is just as meticulous as ever with his control of the vehicle. He does his mirror checks, indicates, and then turns into the road which leads towards my cul-de-sac.

Something seems different, but I can't quite put my finger on it.

I turn back to AA, confident that he knows the way to my house well enough from here on in . . . he's broken into it enough times . . .

"I was wondering if I could stay with you for a while."

AA manages to get out that unbreakable chain of comprehension.

No stuttering, no slurring, it's almost as if he's channelled the same steely nerve he possesses with his drink-driving.

I feel my whole body revolt at the idea.

The hair sticks up on the back of my neck, my throat suddenly dries up, and I feel a tingle pass both through my healed ribcage and my shot-through calf muscle.

"What happened to your place?" I say.

AA slips me another of his glances, and then faces forwards once more.

It's a look which tells me, *Never mind.*

As AA rounds the corner of the street, turning into my cul-de-sac, I can't shake the feeling that something *is* totally and completely wrong.

And it's only then that I see what it is.

Smoke.

Flames.

Fire.

When my eyes slink across the façades of the houses, and to my own home, I see that it's ablaze. Fire belching from every conceivable crevice.

If AA says something to me, I don't hear it.

I stab down on the Release button of my seatbelt.

Leap out of the car.

Chapter Five

M Y HEART DOESN'T SEEM to hit a single beat as I
limbo down under the police tape which cordons off
the cul-de-sac. People are out of their homes, in their pyjamas,
staring at the flames as they soar higher and higher into the
night sky.

The drizzle seems like an afterthought now, because although
it continues to fall, it does nothing to quell the flames. I can hear
a faint *sizzle* as it makes contact with the fire.

A fire engine sits askance in the middle of the road.

Firefighters stand in my front garden, a hose sagging between
them.

A couple of police cars bookend the scene, their blue-and-red
lights swilling about, setting the whole street in almost
pantomime-style lighting.

"Madam, *madam*—excuse me, madam!"

I hear the voice but I pay no attention.

Not until I feel the firm grip on the sleeve of my fake fur coat.

It's then that I turn, reluctantly, away from the bellowing flames consuming my home. Consuming what's *mine*.

I see the stern, flour-white expression staring back at me. A policewoman. Her hair tucked into a business-like bun beneath her pillbox hat. Her frumpy, well-padded jacket making her seem about twice the size she truly is.

When I try to break away from her, she holds on tight.

"Please, madam, stay back behind the cordon."

Even though I know I must sound pathetic, I can't help uttering the words. "My home," I say, "that's my *home*."

"I'm sorry, madam, you're going to have to step over here. It's not safe."

It's as if everything moves in slow motion.

I feel the thoughts and feelings pass through my brain—one by one.

My possessions within.

My cat Lizzie within.

It's the second which leads me to break away from the policewoman.

I do it just like the kids in the movies, slipping my arms out of my coat, and rushing towards the flames, dressed now only in flat shoes and my cocktail dress. I feel the drizzle turn to rivulets and run along the surface of my smooth skin.

As I run faster, get closer to the firemen, all of them dressed in their faded, yellow uniforms, their rugged helmets with torches strapped to the crown, I can taste the ash layering at the back of my throat. It only spurs me on.

I hit the ground harder.

Someone shouts out to me, but I ignore their words.

Before anybody else can grab hold, I'm already passing through the side gate, and headed for my back garden. Once I stand in my back garden, I can't help a dizzy smile, thinking about how easy it really was for AA to break into my house all those times.

I never even locked the side gate.

Smoke pumps out over the garden: thick and black, rendering my house almost impossible to see.

It makes planning my entrance harder still.

My gaze drops down, to the French doors before me.

Within, beneath the level of the smoke, I can see my cat —*Lizzie*—pawing at the glass, her miaows silenced by the double glazing.

I try to open the French doors, squeeze the release button on the latch.

Nope, locked.

I swear to myself, stamp my foot out of frustration. But then my mind flashes back to being rational. Logical thinking kicks in once more.

I look around me, spot a discarded half brick lying in an untended flowerbed.

I grab for it, my thoughts coming so quickly that they're dizzying.

I'm aware of someone else shouting out at me.

Someone staring at me from the side alley I just passed through.

I don't hear them, though, as I bring the brick down—*hard*—against the glass.

And then again—*and again*—until I manage to bust a hole large enough to slip my arms through.

Lizzie leaps into my arms and, as I draw her back out, I'm only dimly aware of the dull pain in my right hand as it scrapes along the broken glass.

And then someone else's arms are around me.

Drawing me away.

Chapter Six

F OR THE LONGEST TIME, I lose myself in Lizzie's contented purr as I hold her in my arms. I stand back from my house, outside the taped-off area, playing by fire department and police rules.

"Madam?"

I glance up, see that the same policewoman from before, the one who tried to take me away from the scene, is standing before me. "Yes?" I say.

"Do you think you could answer a few questions?"

I look into her eyes, see the underlying sternness there. Although I try my best not to make snap judgements about people—those tend to get you into *all sorts* of trouble—I get the impression from her short hair, the dark circles beneath her eyes, a grey hair or two, all those indicators of premature ageing, that she's a single mother; two, maybe three, kids at home.

"What'd you need to know?" I say, looking back at my house,

to the fire fighters now trawling through the wreckage, smoke smouldering up into the night-time sky.

The ash still hangs thick in the air. I believe that I can feel it actually *clogging* my pores as I stand on the street. But I tell myself that's impossible.

That surely I'm not *that* sensitive.

The policewoman meets my eye, and follows my gaze back to my now-decrepit looking home. "I'm sorry about your house," she says, then looks back at me with her lips pressed tightly together, a slight frown embedded in her forehead. "I take it you have insurance?"

I feel my heart thrum in my throat, and then lurch about at this woman's less-than-sympathetic manner. But I hold myself back, give Lizzie a little squeeze to calm me down, telling myself that I'm in a highly sensitised state.

I'm not seeing things as well as I might.

I nod in reply to the policewoman's question about insurance, but then I feel something nagging at the back of my brain. I meet the policewoman's eye and say, "The documentation—it was in a filing cabinet, back in the . . ."

"It's okay," the policewoman says, cutting me off, "your company will have their own records, it shouldn't be a problem to work out." From the top pocket of her uniform jacket, the police-woman produces a notepad.

I feel myself dizzily wondering if it's still standard prac-tice—*in the twenty-first century*—for all bobbies to carry notepads.

Apparently it is, at least with *this* bobby.

"Mrs Harris?" the policewoman says.

Just hearing my own name sends a tingling sensation through my ribcage, and then through my shot-up calf muscle. Actually, it's more the tone of *how* the policewoman says it than the fact of hearing my name itself.

"That's your name?" the policewoman repeats.

"*Ms* Harris, yes," I reply, and then, "Where am I going to sleep tonight?"

The policewoman gives a slight smirk—or what I *take* to be a smirk—and then she turns her attention back down to her notepad. "*Ms* Harris," she says, this time emphasising the *Ms* part, "do you have any enemies you're aware of?"

I knit my eyebrows together.

Look back at the policewoman.

" 'Enemies' ?" I say. "What'd you mean?"

The policewoman flips over a few pages of her notepad, apparently searching for a clean one. She produces a pencil from somewhere—I don't get a chance to see *exactly* where. "Yes," the policewoman says, "anybody who you think might wish to harm you?"

I scowl in response, look back to my house. "You think this was arson?"

The policewoman shakes her head. "No, Mrs Harris," she says, and then glances around, perhaps looking for nervous neighbours watching on . . . most of them, though, are concentrating on the firemen doing their work to dampen down my home. "The Bomb Squad have just got through with the scene."

"The *Bomb* Squad?" I say, hardly having the air to get out the words.

Lizzie squirms in my arms, sticks me with a claw. I realise that I'm squeezing her as tightly as I might squeeze a soft toy. I let up with my squeezing and Lizzie rewards me with another few rounds of purrs . . . I guess my heroic act of saving her from a burning building has earned me some Good Will credit.

"Yes," the policewoman says, her eyes lingering over Lizzie, in my arms, "an explosive device was the cause of the fire."

I look the policewoman back in the eye, unable quite to believe what she's saying.

"It failed," the policewoman continues, "the explosive material never ignited, but the fuse ended up starting the fire." She flaps her hand vaguely over her shoulder to indicate my house: now only smouldering ash and sooty brickwork. "We had the Bomb Squad on hand, looking for any other devices, but they couldn't find anything suspicious."

My heart skips several beats as I wait for the policewoman to add an 'except' . . . and to go on with telling me that they *did* find one of the many handguns I have concealed about the premises:

Very much *illegally* held.

But if they did find them, the policewoman says nothing.

"All the same," she says, a slight sigh in her voice as if all this talk of the Bomb Squad has got her ready for bedtime, "we're going to have a few experts in over the following hours—over the next few days—to try and find out whether there *is* anything to be worried about." She glances up, looks over the street. "Don't want anything going off with a street full of people, do we?"

Realising that she's staring at me, I answer, "No," although I later realise that the question was—*most likely*—a rhetorical one.

The policewoman holds a pencil now, over a fresh page of her notebook.

She meets my eye, cocks her head to one side and says, "So, Mrs Harris, any enemies that you can think of?"

Chapter Seven

I GET THROUGH with the policewoman in about five minutes flat, although I can't help but get the impression that she's a *long* way from being done with me, and that there'll be more questions in the coming days.

With Lizzie still in my arms, I trudge on past the neighbours —in their dressing gowns, and with their gawping expressions, watching the end of the drama for the evening . . . or the early morning.

At least it's given them something to talk about at breakfast.

As I plod on towards AA's car—where AA parked up at the end of the road—I hear a voice calling out to me at my heels.

Lizzie squirms about in my arms and then, administering me a let-me-down bite to the back of my hand, I adhere to her request.

I watch as Lizzie trots neatly up to the person who called out to me.

My neighbour—Mrs Pietersen.

She appears just as she always seems to be frozen in my mind. While other people have a habit of going on their merry way and changing up their appearance from time to time, Mrs Pietersen *always* matches my memory of her. Which is to say that, tonight, she's wearing a shapeless dress, a pair of Crocs on her white-socked feet. Her skin is weathered and she has the look of a woman who might be anywhere between sixty and eighty years old.

As she lifts Lizzie up into her arms, I catch a whiff of Mrs Pietersen's lavender perfume. Although it can be somewhat over-powering indoors, I find that it's somewhat refreshing out here, in the street, with smoke from my burned-down house still coiling through the air.

She pads up to me, a half smile stitched onto her lips, Lizzie rubbing the top of her head against the underside of Mrs Pietersen's chin. As Mrs Pietersen comes closer, she gives me a shake of her head. "Almost gave me a heart attack, they did," she says. "Getting that knock on my door—they must've realised that I disconnected my doorbell when they didn't get a response. Thought it was a bunch of yobbos, trying to break in and steal my TV." She takes a step closer to me, then gives me a wink. "Even had my keepsake in my hand when I went to answer the door, the banging was so insistent."

I manage to muster a smile at Mrs Pietersen's choice of words. This 'keepsake' she refers to is nothing less than her deceased husband's service pistol . . . an item which, I'm sure, has been a warming comfort for an elderly widow like Mrs Pietersen on even the coldest of nights.

Mrs Pietersen switches to a hardy expression—a *steely* smile. "I'm so sorry, Anna," she says, "about your home."

I feel my heart sink almost right down to my stomach.

The news hasn't quite hit home with me yet.

My brain hasn't quite managed to get the message that this is *real*—that this has actually *happened*.

"I'm just glad you're okay," I say, and really mean it.

Although I've hardly had a moment to reflect on the implications of my house fire—between the cat-saving heroics, and the grilling by the policewoman—only now do I think about all the other people who live on my street.

Guess that makes me an awful person, right?

Or, at the very least, a *selfish* person . . .

"You have no idea," Mrs Pietersen continues, now rubbing Lizzie's belly, and bringing her out in wave-upon-wave of purrs. "I was worried sick. How the flames were bursting out of the windows—I was certain you were trapped inside, and that you would never be able to escape."

I give her a hardy smile in return, a little touched that Mrs Pietersen clearly cares so deeply about my welfare.

Mrs Pietersen continues, "And then, after the fire brigade showed up, the bomb disposal teams, and—well—I thought I was going to have a *second* heart attack, you know, after that banging at my front door."

"I guess it's been quite a night," I say, and then, realising that the cordoned-off section of the street also includes Mrs Pietersen's house, add, "Where're you going to be staying tonight?"

Mrs Pietersen gives me an easy smile. "It's all right," she says, "Ursula should be by in a shake or two, they've said that they can give me a bed for as long as it takes."

I feel a warming sensation down in the pit of my gut.

I think back to Mrs Pietersen's involvement with the Winged Women charity—an organisation which takes in women looking

to flee their domestic circumstances; women who need somewhere to hide out for a while. And then I think about how *I*
shamelessly abused their service for my own ends . . . then try to
tell myself it was really okay because of that generous donation I
direct debited them once the dust had settled.

Mrs Pietersen becomes distracted all of a sudden. Her gaze
floats up to my head, and then over it. "Oh," Mrs Pietersen says,
a nervous smile tugging at her lips, "there she is now—there's
Ursula now."

When I meet Mrs Pietersen's gaze, I see, sure enough, that
Ursula has arrived, in all her androgynous glory. Just as she was
when she turned up to whisk me away to Winged Women, I see
that she's driving a white four-by-four. I meet Ursula's gaze for
just a second, and see that she's wearing that same cap with a
visor—the one which valets wear in films.

The same men's jacket with sturdy shoulder pads.

Mrs Pietersen glances back at me, gives me a consolatory
smile. "Anna," she says, "if there's anything you need at all then
you're only to ask." She hands me back Lizzie—apparently
confused by the turn of events—and then makes off towards the
parked-up car. She glances back over her shoulder, then makes
the gesture of a phone with her hand.

I watch on as Mrs Pietersen gets into the passenger side of
the four-by-four.

The engine of the four-by-four grumbles loud and long as the
car disappears around the corner and into the night.

I breathe out a steady breath, then set off to go and find AA.

———

AA's right where I left him, in the car. And I notice, right away, that the passenger door is still wide open. And that the engine's still running. I suppose that AA's had just as much of a torrid time in working out how to switch off the car as he had trying to switch it on. When I draw closer still, feeling Lizzie curling up against my chest in my arms, apparently deciding that it's time for her to turn in for the night, I notice that AA's car bumper is neatly pressed up against the one of the car in front.

I feel a quiver pass through my stomach, and glance back to the many—*many*—police cars still parked up in the road, the officers standing about the cordon, keeping nosy neighbours at bay.

When I bend down and look into the car, I see that AA's fallen asleep, pressing his head inelegantly up against the driver's window. He snores away loudly, his feet stretched out beneath him, into the driver's footwell.

I roll my eyes then slump down in the passenger seat with Lizzie in my lap.

I wait a minute or so, just trying to get my thoughts straight, before reaching out and giving him a tap on the arm to wake him up.

Chapter Eight

I N THE END, I decide to take the wheel, realising that it'll be better if I get done for driving without proper insurance than AA driving whilst intoxicated *and* unconscious.

My good deed for the year.

Because we have nowhere to go, and AA can only speak to me in apparently disjointed phrases between five-minute long periods of sleep, I drive us off to a budget motorway hotel about twenty minutes away from my house.

I check myself in at the desk and wonder whether I should wake AA up.

On balance, I decide that he looks perfectly happy slotted into the passenger seat of his car, and since I'm clearly going to be the one picking up the hotel bill, it'll be nice to save the forty-odd quid AA's own room will cost.

I wrap Lizzie up in a clean bath towel I find in the back of AA's car, and carry her through reception with the staff, no doubt, believing that I'm bringing in a baby.

I didn't think it wise to enquire whether or not the hotel was pet friendly.

The bedroom is just about as anonymous as I might've hoped —twin beds, clean, and the toilet seat is wrapped in a plastic lining. I let Lizzie go, allow her to scope out her new surroundings . . . what's probably going to be 'home' for a little while.

I give myself a quick—*hot*—shower and then, because I have nothing else to get dressed in, I put on what I was wearing before: my black cocktail dress. Only breathing in the ash and smoke once again, staring at myself in the mirror, do I wonder whether I should make a habit of leaving a 'getaway' bag somewhere accessible; a change of clothes, toothbrush, etcetera, within.

With nothing else to be done for the night, tucked in under the blankets, and, with Lizzie pawing at the bedspread, making herself comfortable, I click out the light and try to grab some sleep.

———

I'm woken by a ringing phone close—*too close*—to my head.

At first, because I'm still delirious from sleep, I believe that it's my mobile phone, neglecting the fact that I *always* have it switched to vibrate-only. And that it remains tucked into the inside pocket of my fur coat, currently hanging off the back of a chair across the room.

I shift about beneath my covers, finally catching sight of the perpetrator, the phone which sits on my bedside table. I see that there's also a flashing red light accompanying each of the rings. I reach out, grab the handset, then press the speaker to my ear.

"Hello?" I say, my voice sounding muffled and knackered even to my own hearing.

A distant-sounding voice, apparently from down at reception, tells me that there's a man who wishes to come up. I decide, on the balance of things, that it's most probably AA, and so I grant the request. Then I hang up.

I glance about the room, realising that I failed to draw the curtains before going to bed the night before. A permanently, semi-transparent netted curtain, though, did provide me some sort of privacy.

I spy Lizzie, at the foot of my bed, snoring away. Her ears twitching as she dreams her little cat dreams. I prise myself out from beneath my bedding, swivel around and land the soles of my feet down on the too-thin, concrete-hard carpet.

My mouth still tastes strongly of ash, and I can smell the smoke *everywhere* in the room, as if I've hosted my very own barbecue here. Often I've wondered about cleaning ladies at hotels and the deeply unpleasant messes they've no doubt been compelled to tidy up . . . I'll bet that a stink of smoke is among the more common 'messes' as guests negate to follow the Smoking Ban.

There's a pair of—*quite restrained*—knocks at the hotel room door.

I give a yawn, stretch my arms up to the ceiling and then pad over.

I peer through the spyhole, just to be certain . . . *sure enough* there's AA.

Standing in the corridor outside.

A sizeable suitcase in his hand.

He looks extremely crumpled—and not a little *seedy*—in his suit from the night before. I can see that his shirt has become untucked and that his hair sticks out at all sorts of angles he normally does his level best to prevent with the aid of gel.

I put AA out of his misery, and unlatch the door.

"Morning," I say.

AA fixes me with a scowl and paces past me, into the hotel room. He dumps his suitcase down at the door, almost landing it right on top of one of my bare feet. "You left me down in my car —*all night*," he says.

"You didn't notice," I say. "You passed out back on my street."

AA doesn't reply here, or make any mention of the fact that he only realised he'd been sleeping all night in his car a matter of minutes ago. He glances to Lizzie, the scowl still fixed on his face. Then he glances back at me. "Well, guess he survived the fire."

"He's a *she*," I reply.

AA rolls his eyes, then sets about unbuttoning his shirt. As he flashes a little flesh at me, I can't help but notice that the previously firm abdomen has—how should I put this?—come a little undone over the past few weeks.

I guess that AA's been unable to keep up his gym payments, not to mention his personal trainer.

"Gonna take a shower," AA says, grabbing one of the folded-up towels, then sauntering past me into the ensuite bathroom.

Before I have any chance to present an opinion, the door slams shut in my face.

As AA showers, the dripping sound of water a strangely calming influence on the room, I flip on the TV—half expecting to see that my house fire has made the national news. It hasn't, of course, despite the bomb crews showing up.

And that makes me all the more suspicious.

Suspicious that Brian Mathewson had something to do with this.

He who controls the media controls the world . . .

Approximately fifteen minutes later, AA emerges from the bathroom—*thankfully*—with a towel wrapped around his waist. I catch that thick, musky scent of well-soaped man, and I sneak myself a tiny smile at AA's slightly flabby waistline.

AA doesn't see my smirk.

Holding his towel to his waist with one hand, he stoops over the suitcase, knocking it down flat with a single strike.

I'm guessing that somebody's not exactly feeling like roses this morning . . .

He snaps open the catches then digs through the clutter within, the heaps—*and heaps*—of screwed-up clothes. He mumbles to himself as he goes about selecting his wardrobe for the day, and I can't help saying, "You know, talking to yourself is the first sign of madness."

He either doesn't hear me, or he mumbles something offensive under his breath.

Finally, AA straightens himself up, standing tall again, and he paces over to the desk, laying out what's—*apparently*—to be his outfit for the day.

From what I can see, it consists of a blue-grey suit jacket—with matching trousers—along with a light-pink shirt. His underwear, I'm a little disappointed to note, is fairly ordinary: white, cotton Y-fronts with matching socks.

Both look to be in good condition, too.

I don't know that I've ever really given the matter a great deal of conscious thought, but I believe that I've always painted AA, in my mind, as either wearing outrageously saucy underwear, or being a closet slob . . . using underwear and socks covered in holes.

Guess my people-reading skills could do with some work . . .

As AA dresses himself, he tilts his head upwards, to look at the TV screen, the twenty-four-hour news channel I have running. "Anything?" he says, his back to me.

"No," I reply, "nothing that I've seen, anyway."

AA zips up his trousers, slips a belt on and then sets about buttoning his shirt. He looks at me, long and hard, then says, "Have you got it?"

I give a smirk. "Were you really that drunk?"

AA looks about the room, as if he's searching for something. "Is it here?" he says, apparently answering my previous question in the affirmative.

"Yes," I say, "it's in the inside pocket of my coat."

AA's eyes finally come to rest on my coat, still dangling off the back of the chair. Then he nods to himself. "Good," he says, almost to himself. "That's *good*."

I half watch the sports roundup on the TV screen—the luminescent-green football pitch; players jostling about with one another before falling into barely contained ecstasy. Tearing myself away from the screen, I say, out of the corner of my mouth, "When'd you think it's safe to go back?"

"Back where?" AA says, currently distracted by the act of tucking his shirt into his trousers.

"*Home*," I say, then nod to the TV screen, to the non-existent news report there. "When'd you think the police will've scarpered?"

AA glances back at me, meets my eye for a fraction of a second. "Don't know," he replies, and then, "You think they might find something incriminating?"

I give a roll of my eyes, a shake of my head. "Just the small matter of the various handguns lying around—and if they uncover one of my bank statements then I guess there might be some questions to answer about those irregular—*large*—payments from Mathewson Media, don't you think?"

AA continues to stare at me, apparently distracted by something else on his mind.

"What?" I say. "What is it?"

"You should be set for a bumper insurance pay-out, right?"

I feel my chest tighten. A tingle passes through my ribs. "Uh, *hopefully*," I say, "as long as my policy isn't invalidated by undetonated bombs . . ."

It's clear, from AA's expression, that he thinks that this is some sort of ill-judged joke. I make a note to explain the situation to him more clearly later on, but, right now, with that stench of smoke and ash covering near enough everything, I can't quite summon the energy.

Finally, I settle on, "Yes—I'm insured out of my arse."

A smile appears on AA's lips. "Good," he says, "that's good."

"Tell me about it."

AA's attention gradually drifts back to the TV screen, and then, as if an idea has just struck him—or a bolt of electricity has run up his spine—he turns to me and says, "Shopping?"

Chapter Nine

I DECIDE that it'd be silly to run the baby routine with Lizzie again—to wrap her up in a blanket so that I can sneak her through reception. So, instead, I settle on leaving her behind in the hotel room, hanging up one of those laminated DO NOT DISTURB signs on the doorknob.

Hopefully that'll keep the cleaners honest.

Before me and AA venture out of the room, I leave the bathroom taps running just a smidge, and watch on as Lizzie bounds up onto the rim of the bath to watch, before, quite happily, licking at the constantly falling fresh water.

"We'll need cat food," I say to AA as we pass through the automatic double doors of the hotel, out into the car park, and towards AA's waiting and—*in daylight*—quite ostentatious yellow sports car.

I don't think to ask if AA's okay to drive the morning-after-the-night-before, and hope that the breakfast we slipped down our throats—along with *lashings* of coffee for AA—will have had some effect on the alcohol surely still bombing about AA's bloodstream.

AA drives us back into London, to Notting Hill.

Although AA insists on dragging me into some designer boutiques, I manage to sneak us into some charity shops, too; so that I can pick up some bits and pieces: simple things that I really don't need to be stretching my budget for.

I can't help but feel that I'm getting some strange looks off people, browsing the shops on a Saturday morning while wearing a fur coat, and my cocktail dress from the night before on underneath. And perhaps I bow to this pressure after the first hour or so of browsing as I opt to change into a pair of no-nonsense tracksuit bottoms, and a fleecy jumper on top; both of which I picked up from a charity shop.

My changing magic done, me and AA continue to go about town picking up a few extras. And despite AA's penchant for ordinary underwear himself, he attempts to swing me into buying some sexy undies.

I pay little attention.

Once we've finished up our shopping—and we've landed to have a coffee; guess who's buying?—I turn my attention to my mobile phone.

I see that I have a message from my boyfriend, Mark:

What're you up to tonight?

My heart leaps a touch as I see his name written out on the screen. I can't help feeling a little guilty that I haven't yet told him about my house burning down.

I excuse myself from the table, leaving AA to make puppy-dog eyes at the attractive male barista—blond and in his teens, just how AA likes them.

I head out of the café; to the street outside.

People pass me by, mothers with children in tow, bearing shopping bags, looking thoroughly fed-up with it all. Groups of men wearing football shirts and jeans, apparently carefree and —*most likely*—a little tipsy before heading to their football stadiums of choice. And then there're the old couples, silver-haired and plodding along, without any sense of rush.

Everyone is wrapped up in a winter coat. Their breath forms clouds as it exits their mouth.

I can hear a man with an out-of-tune acoustic guitar—and an *even more* out-of-tune singing voice—yelping his way through a rock classic that I can't seem to recall the name of right now.

I'm dying for a drink of water after the bitter, foamy coffee I just downed with AA, and, despite everything, I can still smell the strong scent of smoke and ash clinging to me, even though I've cast off the clothes I wore the night before.

Maybe I'll have to incinerate those clothes.

Once I've tapped away at the contacts list on my phone, and having finally settled on Mark's name, I punch the Call button and hold the handset up to my ear. When the yelping busker gets too much, I stick a finger in my other ear, so that I can better make out the burbling call signal.

Mark answers me after three or four rings.

"Anna?"

Despite myself—despite everything that's occurred in the past twelve hours, I find myself smiling to just hear his voice . . . perhaps it *is* love after all. "Mark? Hi, how're you?"

Mark seems occupied with something in the background.

I can't help but imagine him at home, in his workshop,

crafting something immaculate out of wood—because that's what he does to earn a living; he's an 'ornamental' carpenter.

"Fine," he replies finally, sounding almost as if he's at the bottom of a well. "You got my message, then?"

I stare out across the bustling crowds—the people all packed together, and despite their differently coloured clothes, all the effort they make to stand out, I can't shift the idea that they're all moving together as one. Marching together as one. To the same drumbeat . . . or, perhaps, to the busker's out-of-tune strummings.

"Yeah," I say, and then, "About that, about tonight."

"What is it?" Mark replies, and despite the dampened sound quality on his end of the call, I can hear the hurt.

Not seeing any other way to break what's happened to me lightly, I just blab it out.

There's a long pause while Mark absorbs what I've said.

"Your house burned down?" he says.

"Yes," I reply, surprising myself that I'm *smiling*.

"I . . . uh, is everything okay . . . are *you* okay?"

"Fine," I say, "and it seems like none of my neighbours came to any harm either." I toy with the idea of adding the extra information and decide that there's no harm to it. "I was with AA, last night, I went out for a drink. When I came back the house was burning down."

Another long pause on Mark's end of the line.

I've illustrated, quite clearly, and on many occasions, exactly what AA is . . . taken great pains in demonstrating that our relationship isn't so much as like brother and sister as like dog and master—though who's the dog and *who's* the master at any one time sometimes gets mixed up.

It seems that there's likely to be only *one* solution to this uneasiness in my and Mark's relationship: I'm going to have to introduce him to AA.

Just the idea of it makes me shudder.

Brings me out in a cold sweat.

When Mark's voice comes again, it's cleaner, *smoother*. It sounds as if somebody's tossed him a rope so that he can drag himself out of whatever hole he was stuck down—though I suppose, in reality, he's actually just stepped out of his workshop and into the fresh air on this sunny, if a little nippy, Saturday morning.

"Do you need me to do anything?" he says.

I arch an eyebrow, although there's little chance of that particular gesture being communicated down the line . . . why *is* it that men are always looking to pitch in with some sort of 'solution' ?

When one's house goes and burns down one thing is for certain—there's going to be an awful lot of waiting; a lot of patience exercised; before things can return to normal.

In the end, I just tell Mark that I'm coping fine, and that I'll speak with him later on.

Then I turn my attention back to the café—peer in through the window.

And—*sure enough*—I see AA, leaning casually on the glass counter, chatting bullshit to the rather fetching male barista . . . and being thoroughly rebuffed.

Maybe I should throw AA a few quid so he can get his personal trainer back.

Or at least so that he can get in the door at the gym. And get to work on recovering that famed washboard stomach of his.

Chapter Ten

BACK IN THE HOTEL ROOM, I take stock of my purchases.

Lizzie, stirred from her nap, and apparently looking for some diversion, paws her way through the various garments I've purchased. She soon locates the cat food—I don't know quite how she recognises the packaging—and she rubs her body up against it.

Deciding that she probably *is* in need of some breakfast, I make use of the dainty porcelain soap dish in the bathroom to pour out Lizzie's food.

Lizzie flattens her body against the ground, lays her tail to rest behind her, and tucks into her breakfast; me and AA apparently, at least for the time being, forgotten.

I take another shower to get the ash-and-smoke stench off me.

In the end, I do decide to throw out the dress and fur coat I used the night before. And although I'm sad to watch AA drop them inside a black plastic bag, I know that it's for the better. Somebody with more patience—and with an accessible washing machine—might make a good fist of using them.

After I'm done organising, as best as I can, my clothes in the wardrobe of the hotel room, me and AA each take up a position, one of us on each twin bed. We lie back watching TV . . . the news again, and—*still*—no word about the bomb at my house.

I can't help but perform some mental gymnastics, thinking about how much Brian Mathewson might've paid to my neighbours to keep them quiet.

I'm thankful to observe, though, that my face doesn't flash up on screen as part of some ongoing police enquiry—that I've not been made a fugitive now that they've turned up some 'suspicious materials' at my house.

When I check my phone, I see that I have several missed calls from unknown numbers. I assume that it's the police trying to get in touch. No doubt they need me to be present at the scene while they go through the premises looking for other probable causes of the fire.

I don't really have the stomach for an investigation.

Truth be told, more than anything, I just want to slip back there, see if there's anything worth salvaging, then take the insurance money and set about starting again.

That's if AA's ongoing life expenses—let alone the six-figure *loan*—will leave me pocket change from the insurance pay-out to purchase another home.

Once we've been lying about on our respective beds for about an hour, and in that time Lizzie has ordered two further servings of food—no doubt citing trauma—I turn to AA and say, "Want me to get you a room of your own?"

AA wrinkles his nose, and continues to stare at the TV screen. "Nah," he says. "No point, is there?"

I'm a little taken aback by the confidence of this answer—I *am* the one paying for the comparative luxury of a hotel room versus the back seat of his car, after all.

"Don't know," I say, "thought you might like some privacy."

AA shifts his weight on his bed, slips me a sidelong glance. "You're staying at Mark's, so it'd be a bit silly for you to get *another* room here."

Despite everything—despite being *well* into my thirties—I can't stop myself from blushing a touch . . . *Jesus*, it's like it's the nineteenth century all over again . . .

"No," I say, "I'm not."

AA gives a wide smirk—one of those deeply *arrogant* smirks which just drives me crazy, which makes me want to throttle him. But I hold myself back, knowing that I have to conserve my energy for the time being. "Trust me," AA says, his attention still exclusively focussed on the TV screen. "This time tomorrow you will be."

I snuggle up tight to Lizzie and try to forget AA's there at all.

Chapter Eleven

I ARRIVE at Mark's house that evening, around six.

He called me back in the middle of the afternoon and it was all I could do—in my desperation to get away from AA for a few hours—not to *beg* him to have me.

He seemed somewhat surprised that I wasn't all busy with the house fire, but I assured him that I'd spoken with the police, and they'd—*in turn*—told me that I wouldn't be required on the scene for another few days.

That was a lie, of course.

I've been dodging the unknown-number phone calls all day.

I turn up to Mark's wearing a strappy top beneath a denim coat. And I can't help but feel the wintery chill clinging to the air. It seems to almost slice right through me as I stand on his doorstep, waiting for him to come to the door.

My thoughts turn to nostalgia when I think about the fur coat which me and AA took the executive decision to chuck out just that afternoon . . . already I'm regretting it.

When Mark does come to the door, he's dressed in a checked shirt, untucked, over a pair of well-worn-in jeans. He has his black hair drawn back in a ponytail, as I imagine he wears it when he's putting in Hard Graft in his workshop.

His hazel eyes send a thrill through me.

He takes a step inside, inviting me in, almost timid in his movements.

I soon sort *that* out as I lean hard into him and plant a kiss right *smack* on his lips.

And I can't prevent my curious hands from wandering all over his rock-hard body, across his ripped stomach, and down to his smooth, firm thighs.

"Where's Nathan?" I say, referencing Mark's adopted son . . . and one of my own son—Ben's—contemporaries at school . . . I'd say *friend* except I don't think that I've ever seen the two of them hanging out; not since we took a joint camping trip a while back.

Mark tilts his head to one side, gives a faint smile. "At a friend's house," he says.

Already, as I take another step into the house, I can breathe in the divine scent of garlic and onions cooking—something with a spicy bite there, too, also thrown into the culinary mix.

Mark's kitchen puts mine to shame . . . or it *did* when my kitchen was still in existence.

It features lightly coloured blue-green tiles and oak(?) floorboards.

In place of three of the four walls, there are wide windows which look out into the garden.

At the moment, it being winter, Mark has all the windows shut tight. But I can tell that in summer it must be otherworldly to cook late into the evenings.

Hopefully I'll stick around long enough to *see* Mark's house in summer . . .

I'm not too good at long-term relationships, although I seem to be doing *okay* with this one.

So far.

"What's cooking?" I say, hooking my thumbs into the back pockets of my jeans.

"Oh, just a stir-fry sort of thing, I was thinking."

I glance back at Mark—ever the self-deprecating one. "Go on," I say. "You can say its name, I won't think you're a nerd or anything."

A smile twitches the corner of Mark's mouth. "It's Moo Goo Gai Pan," he says.

"*Nerd*," I reply, skulking a little more about the kitchen, taking time to stare at this or that.

Mark just has so many interesting trinkets about the place. I stop beside a teacup tree, look over the wooden struts which Mark hand carved himself . . . in Mark's house, it's a fairly decent bet that anything that's wood has come about from *his* personal involvement.

Over my shoulder, I hear a *hiss* as Mark tosses in some olive oil. "So," Mark says, "you don't seem too traumatised by this whole house-burning-down thing?"

I feel a slight shudder pass over the surface of my skin. The truth is, with the speed at which everything has happened, I haven't really had the opportunity to decide *how* I do feel about it.

"Yeah, well," I say, "I was thinking of making some changes —I guess the fire just gave me a kick over the edge."

I lean up against the smooth kitchen counter, which is made of a wood which, I'm sure if I asked, Mark would tell me the origin and age of . . . and what exactly he did to make it feel so smooth beneath my touch.

For a long while, we just stand in his kitchen, the two of us in silence, me observing him at work at his gas stove, stirring the contents of the frying pan with a wooden spatula which has an ornately carved zebra's head at one end.

The fact that *even I* can tell it's a zebra is surely testament to Mark's skill.

I just absorb the wonderful smells of the cooking chicken puffing through the air, and then the dry scent of mushrooms. All of those details make me forget about everything that's happened in the past twenty-four hours, and I even stop my worrying about the misadventures AA and Lizzie are surely experiencing back in the hotel.

After about five minutes of silence, Mark turns to me, gives me one of his *gorgeous* smiles, and then says, "I didn't ask if you wanted a glass of wine."

And, although I don't *usually*, for Mark I say yes.

———

It's around two in the morning when AA is finally proven right.

And, if he was here, in Mark's house with me right at this moment, I'd strangle him quite happily.

As me and Mark lie back in his deliciously soft featherbed—a *welcome* change from the hard hotel mattress from the night before—I run my hands across his furry belly, tangling his wiry, black hairs up with my fingertips.

Mark's adopted son, Nathan, is staying over at his friend's house tonight, so me and Mark have taken full advantage of having the house to ourselves. Having the kitchen, the sitting room, the dining room . . . Mark's workshop . . . all to *ourselves*.

All tired out, Mark lies with his hands tucked back behind his head, his attention drawn very much upwards, to the skylight.

When I follow his gaze, I see that there's hardly a cloud in the sky tonight, and that there're cascades of twinkling stars, the names of which—*even their constellations*—I don't dare to even think about for fear of getting them hilariously wrong.

"Anna?" Mark says.

"Mm hmm," I reply, hypnotised by the stars above us for a few seconds.

"If it's no trouble, would you like to move in with me?"

I feel a pang right down in the pit of my stomach. One of those pangs which can either happen because it's something good, or it's something *very* bad.

But which is it this time?

As I lie there, absorbing Mark's words, he backtracks slightly, "Just until you've sorted out your own house, of course." He pauses for a moment—for a *long* moment—which makes me think that, already, he's regretting having put this offer to me. "It's just, to think that you're living in a hotel, it's just . . . I don't know, a little sad?"

I press my lips together. Give a nod which Mark can't see.

He's right, of course.

And what he doesn't realise is that I'm currently sharing a hotel room with AA.

That would surely push him towards *demanding* that I move in with him.

There's a long—*yearning*—silence between the two of us while the gravity of Mark's statement has a chance to ferment; to take on a form all of its own.

To create its individual meaning for the two of us.

Finally, I decide, realising that *something* needs to be decided at this point. When I turn to him, manoeuvring my chest on top of his, I say, "You're not allergic to cats, are you?"

Chapter Twelve

THE SMUGNESS seems to pour from every one of AA's pores as I set about clearing up the room, packing away my things into the plastic bags I acquired during my shopping spree. I didn't think to purchase any suitcases while me and AA were out shopping—I didn't think *that* far ahead.

AA stands silhouetted at the hotel room window, Lizzie purring away in his arms. He strokes her head as if he was some kind of master villain about to explain his genius *unstoppable* plot to a currently incapacitated hero.

"Told you so," AA says, as I fish about beneath the bed, wondering how I managed to lose so many socks after spending only *one* night in the room.

When I get myself back up onto my knees, and I shoot a glance back over at him—and at Lizzie, apparently *greatly* enjoying AA's soft, but firm hands—I say, "You think you could maybe give me a hand? Then, once we're finished with that, help me lug my stuff downstairs? And then—*after that*—drive me over to Mark's?"

AA keeps up his smirk, and continues to hold Lizzie in his arms.

Me and Lizzie are going to have Serious Words when this is all over.

About just *whose* side she's really on.

AA takes a step towards me, but is no closer to stuffing anything into a plastic bag. "And I suppose you're just going to *leave* me here."

Not bothering to so much as glance up at him, I say, "That's the plan."

"Anna?" he says.

This time there doesn't seem to be an option *not* to look up at him.

So I do.

Attention-seekers really do get on my nerves after a while . . .

"What?" I say.

AA draws in a deep breath, and his shoulders rock back. Gently, he lets Lizzie out of his arms, helps her down onto the hotel room floor. "Do you remember what we talked about—the night your house burned down?"

I restrain a sigh. "Yes," I say, "I think I can just about see through my trauma to remembering *that.*"

"Well . . ." AA says, allowing the word to linger.

"Tell you what," I say, "I'll go to reception and put down the money for a week here, how does that sound? Then, once that week's done with, we'll have a chat." I pause for a moment and then, for good measure, flick my hair over my shoulder. "Sound fair?"

AA gives a wince, and then, a sure-fire sign of trying to get on my good side, he crouches down and takes hold of a rogue can of deodorant—slips it inside one of the plastic bags. "The thing is, Anna, I've got some people, well, sort of breathing down my neck?"

"What'd you mean?" I say, feeling my stomach sink. "You mean debt collectors?"

AA rocks his head from side to side in a gesture that can only mean 'yes'. He straightens up then meets my eye once more. "Look," he says, "here's the thing, that figure I talked about, the amount I mentioned, I'm going to need that money by tomorrow, or . . ."

"Or else what?" I say.

"Well," AA's eyes loll about at the top of their sockets as he searches for something on the ceiling . . . "Let's just say that the two of us will be in some serious doo-doo."

That brings my packing to a halt.

I stand firm, feeling Lizzie brush her body up against my calves.

"Like *what*?" I say, my voice firm. "What've *I* got to do with this? Who've you been borrowing money from?"

All of a sudden, I see a twinkle in his eye . . . something which tells me—on a gut level—that maybe all this is a windup. But—if it is—it's not a particularly funny one.

"Do you remember that rather charming stewardess?" he says.

The rage is rising in me now—and it's become so overpowering that I almost need to scrunch my eyes shut to keep it down inside me. "What're you talking about?"

"You know"—he twizzles his fingers in the air as if I'm meant to read between the lines—"*Her*?"

"No," I reply, "I *don't* know. You're going to have to spell it out to me, *very* plainly."

AA winces again, showing off his slightly yellowed teeth.

I guess that he's had to cut back on trips to the hygienist too.

"Tabby," AA says, calmly, succinctly.

Why was *that* so hard?

. . . That's when I start to realise why . . . because I can already feel the anger bubbling up in my stomach. How we promised each other—me and AA—that we would have nothing at all further to do with Brian Mathewson or his associates. That we would watch one another's back. In reality, I should probably be pissed off with AA for my house burning down.

And that's when it clicks.

AA.

My house burning down.

He was responsible for keeping me clear.

For keeping me out of the way.

So that no harm would come to me—but so that *my* house would burn down.

I tilt my head to one side, feeling as if a cog's come loose somewhere in my brain.

"You," I say, stalking towards him. "*You!*"

AA backs up, towards the window.

Only now do I realise that it's open, just a few centimetres. But, surely, just a push—*just one hard push*—would be all it'd take for AA's weight to shove it all the way open.

And to send him sprawling through the air, down onto the concrete car park four storeys below . . . probably enough to kill him, if he lands the wrong way.

AA's shoulders press up against the window behind him. "Please, Anna, you don't understand . . . you don't understand the *circumstances*. A warning, that was all it was. It was hard—almost impossible—"

But he doesn't get the chance to say anything else.

I clock him—*hard*—in the jaw.

I hear a *crunch* but I don't stick around to see if it was bone breaking.

I just turn, grab Lizzie under my arm, take hold of as many plastic bags as I can manage.

Then I head for the hotel room door.

Leave the bastard to bleed on the floor.

Chapter Thirteen

I'M SURPRISED at how calm I manage to act when I reach Mark's house.

I pin on a smile and, after a few moments, find that it doesn't come with too much difficulty.

Mark helps me to lug the plastic bags out of the taxi and in through his front door. His adopted son, Nathan, comes to help me too.

Just like always, Nathan says almost nothing at all. His crop of raven hair and height, as always, causing me to remind myself that he *isn't* Mark's biological son. Today he wears a green-and-white striped retro football shirt . . . which team it corresponds to, I really haven't a clue.

Once we've got everything inside Mark's house, Nathan disappears off to his bedroom, shuts the door. No doubt firing up some video game, like my own son—Ben—is wont to do.

For several long—*awkward*—moments, Mark stands about in his front hall, scratching at the back of his neck. The two of us watch on as Lizzie sniffs about the plastic bags, her body flattened to the front-hall floor tiles, apparently not quite convinced about this whole plan of mine and Mark's for me to move in.

Finally, the spell is broken when she wraps her body up against the leg of Mark's jeans, gives a miniscule *brurr* and slips off in the direction of the kitchen.

No doubt to check if Mark's committed the rookie error of leaving some food out . . . tuna would be most appreciated.

As I move my gaze *above* the waistband of his jeans, I see that today Mark has on a button-up cotton shirt: a beige base material with multi-coloured, thin lines running up it.

As I stand there, I breathe in his thick, musky smell. There's a hint of lemon, or lime, there too, and it sends a slight quiver through my gut. I can't help but notice those bustling muscles, also, and how I'd love to wrap my hands about them.

But not right now. That's one of the disadvantages of kids being about the house during the day. There's little chance for some Afternoon Delight.

"Anna," he says, a gentle smile aimed at me.

"Mark?" I say, setting my hands on my hips and giving him an arched eyebrow back in return.

I can tell—from his tone—that he's about to lay out something which he finds *difficult* to explain.

Mark meets my eye for precisely a quarter of a second, then says, "I was wondering—I thought you'd probably want some of your own space, you know, so I was just thinking . . . if I . . ."

"If you could put me up in the guest room?" I put in, deciding to help out this poor, floundering man.

Mark gives me a weak smile in reply. "Yes," he says, "that's it."

I feel a warm glow grow within my chest; rise up through my

bloodstream. When I meet his eye again, I see that he's gone all straight-faced . . . it gives me the impression that he's really given this some Very *Serious* Thought Indeed.

"Sure," I say, and really mean it.

It'll be nice to have my own space again.

———

About twenty minutes later, I've got everything nicely organised.

I take care with the memory stick, wondering about where I'm going to stash it for safe keeping. In the end, I opt for a spot behind a book in Mark's bookcase—by far the dustiest one there . . . I do this on the pretence that nobody will think to slip it out in the too near future.

That done, I step back to take in the spare room.

It's about half the size of Mark's own bedroom, but that doesn't mean it's unpleasant.

Like Mark's bedroom, there's a skylight, currently giving me a view of the mottled, grey clouds above. Grim weather moving in.

A sleek, white vase sits on the bedside table. There's a collection of yellow and purple flowers within—what their technical names *actually* are will forever remain a mystery to me. But, one thing is for certain, they smell awfully *strong*—they send my nostril hairs tingling.

There're twin beds, both with neat, clean bedding; and both of them without so much as a crease. If there's one thing I've noted about Mark's house, as a whole, it's that he doesn't tolerate disorder gladly.

When I slip off my shoes—and then my socks for good measure—I take several moments to savour the feel of the curly carpet ebbing between my toes. It has that quality which all the very best—the most *luxurious*—of carpets all have . . . it feels almost as if I'm walking upon grass . . . like it supports my weight with its springy texture.

Finally, I come to rest on the edge of the bed, allowing myself to sink down into the slinky, soft mattress. As I sit there, allowing myself to breathe in deep, then—for good measure—exhaling long and hard, I note the gilt-framed artwork hanging from the wall just before my eyes. The picture depicts a natural landscape —a series of lush, green hills with smoky fog drifting all around them, like wispy hair on an elderly man's scalp . . . all right, a particularly *ill* elderly man; one whose skin has gone an *extremely* unnatural colour.

In the foreground of the picture, on the hillsides, I make out the white splodges of sheep grazing. All of them, seemingly, indifferent to what must be incredibly cold weather.

Even with those deep, dark clouds moving in over the hills.

Or perhaps they're just too stupid to notice at all.

To realise the significance of it.

I know the polite thing for me to do—now that I've sorted myself out—would be to go downstairs and make conversation with Mark. But Mark, when he helped me to lug my plastic bags up here, to the spare bedroom, was very clear that I should feel fine about just 'hanging out' in my room . . . having a chance to 'get my thoughts together'.

Mark's kindness and understanding almost makes me want to cry.

It puts my defences up all the more, makes me wonder if— perhaps—he's going to snap at any moment, if he's going to suddenly do or say something which'll show off his real character.

Because nobody can *ever* be *this* nice . . . can they?

My bedroom is located right next to Nathan's.

Through the walls, I can hear the gentle sounds of virtual gunfire—a digitalised scream here and there as Nathan's pretend victims succumb . . .

It *does* seem strange that Nathan and my son, Ben, aren't better friends.

Because they seem to have the same taste in games.

I've just made the decision to rise up off the bed, and have only got to my feet, when I hear the distinct *rumble* of my phone vibrating its way across my bedside table. I tread over to it—check the number there—and see that it's Unknown.

I roll my eyes, wondering if it's AA, calling me up to offer some sort of a cock-eyed explanation for what he's done . . . for his part in burning down my house.

Perhaps the fact that he's calling through an anonymous number shows that he's had time to think—to *realise* the gravity of what he's done.

And perhaps that's what gets me lifting the phone up to my ear.

"Hello?" I say, pressing the handset to the side of my head.

There's a brief pause on the other end, which tells me that, whoever *is* there, is extremely busy, and has been getting some minor task done while waiting for me to pick up.

Then comes the nasal, slightly *snide*, male voice. I can't help but picture, in my mind, a skinny man in a tight-fitting suit; hair slicked back and combed meticulously with gel. Perhaps a pair of round-rimmed spectacles and a moustache, too, to boot. "Yes, hello," he says. "Is this, uh"—he apparently checks some screen or form he has in front of him—"*Anna Harris?*"

"Yes," I say, "that's me."

"Mrs Harris," he says, and I decide not to correct his

marrying me off, "this is Roger Tittlemarth of Sundaze Holdings, I work in the Claims office. Your insurer?" He allows a professional pause—I suppose it's too allow me to process this information through my thick, non-bureaucrat brain. "I understand that you experienced a house fire?"

"That's right," I say, seeing no need to get snarky.

"Right, Mrs Harris," he continues, as if I haven't said anything at all, "I've been looking over the evidence, over the reports we've received from the police, and, from what I've seen here so far, I must inform you that we're in a position to reject your claim outright, before proceeding any further."

Without any conscious effort on my part, I feel my forehead furrow. "I'm sorry, what?"

"Yes, Mrs Harris," he goes on, "it's the belief of Sundaze Holdings that, from the information we've been handed from the police, the source of the fire was by deliberate means . . ." he leaves the sentence lingering as he—*apparently*—checks some detail before him ". . . from an improvised explosive device?"

I don't really know what to say in reply to this.

"Mrs Harris? Are you still there?"

"Yes," I say, feeling a numbness crawl all over my body. It's then that I blink several times, as if clearing a daze that's built up before my eyes. "What . . . what should I do now?"

"Well, Mrs Harris," Roger Tittlemarth says, as if he's reading from a crib sheet or, more likely, has memorised the official statement he should provide claimants. "You will have the opportunity to appeal in writing, of course, to give your side of things . . . although, really, I have a duty to inform you that you'll need to prepare yourself with a *very* tight case indeed, because the evidence we have here, from the police, it's—*well*, for want of a better word—quite *damning*."

"I see," I reply.

Roger Tittlemarth's tone is crisp and clear as he finishes up, "If you have any further questions or queries then please contact us . . ."

But I allow the phone to slip down from my ear as he jabbers away about the number to call in case of the need for assistance.

Yeah, what sort of assistance am I likely to need?

For a long time, I sit slouched on the bed in the spare room of Mark's house, my head spinning. It helps a little when I reach up and apply pressure to my temples. Off, downstairs, I can smell onions, garlic and spices all cooking up, and I know that Sunday dinner's going to be just *incredible*.

If only I could bring myself to make everything else go away.

So that I might enjoy it.

Chapter Fourteen

W HEN WE GET through with Sunday dinner—some sort of an Indian dish that I forget the name of as soon as it leaves Mark's mouth—I expect to have to hang around for some sort of 'interaction' period . . . to, out of politeness, have to make conversation with Mark and Nathan.

Of course that'd be *totally* unreasonable . . .

Thankfully, though, Mark performs his understanding trick again, and, with a gentle smile, tells me that I can quite happily —and *guilt-free*—toddle on up to my bedroom; go rest my head.

When I get there, I find that Lizzie's already made herself quite comfortable on the previously *wrinkle-free* bedspread. She's all stretched out, her eyes half open, and I can tell, from those sidelong glances of hers, that she's expecting me to give her tummy a good rub.

I do that for several minutes, and the trundling vibrations of her purrs passing through my fingertips relaxes me. At least I'm having a positive impact on *some* creature's wellbeing—if only for a matter of moments.

I sit slumped there, on the bed, for a long time.

Just thinking to myself.

I hardly turn a thought to what time it might be when I hear footsteps on the landing outside. The footsteps are soon followed by a knock at my door. I ask them to come in.

It isn't Mark darkening my doorway—as I expected—but *Nathan*.

He gives me one of those nervous early-teenager smiles, then busies himself with the tattered fringes of his jean pockets. "Dad told me to come tell you something," he says.

I give him a warm—*welcoming* . . . at least it *feels* welcoming to me—smile, giving off all the physical signals I can control that he can speak to me about anything.

And yet, at the same time, I'm scared to death.

That he might be coming to me with something *grave* . . . something which I won't be able to help him with at all.

Maybe he's come to ask me about some girl who he likes at school, and whether he should ask her out, or whatever it is that kids *do* these days when caught up in a fledgling romance.

I turn my attention to him.

Nathan looks to Lizzie, lying on my bed. He smiles. "Dad always talked about us getting a dog—he said that once he went full-time with his carpentry, when he was at home more, then we'd get one." He gives a shake of his head. "But we haven't got one yet—now he says that I'll only be around the house for another five years or so, then I'll be off doing my own thing, so there won't be time for me to look after it."

"Your dad's not a dog person?"

Nathan shrugs. "I guess not," he says.

With that comment, the conversation drifts away into silence, and I get the feeling that Nathan hasn't just come to my room to detail out his feelings on having—*or not having*—a dog about the house . . . one thing's for certain, I know for a fact that Lizzie is *extremely* pleased not to have a canine sniffing around . . .

"It's about dreaming," he says, glancing up at me for a fraction of a second.

It catches me by surprise; the suddenness of his words.

Out of nowhere.

As I look over Nathan's face, I see that he has some of his adopted father's tics and expressions about him. It makes me wonder, all over again, about those arguments to do with Nature vs Nurture. I can certainly see the influence which Mark has had over Nathan.

I keep my eyes fixed on him. "What about dreaming?" I say, now deeply worried that this—*really*—won't be anywhere near my area of expertise.

"At nights," he says. "I get these *bad* dreams . . . they're called night terrors."

" 'Night terrors' ?" I say.

"Yes," he replies, "have you heard of them?"

I shake my head.

He gives a slight shrug, and a smile traces his lips for a moment. "They're like violent nightmares"—another shrug—"sometimes I scream out, sometimes I pound my fists against the wall, stamp my feet, you know, stuff like that?"

His eyes rise up to meet with mine, and he gives another sheepish grin.

"Me and Dad," Nathan says, "we thought that it'd be best for me to tell you about them first, so that you didn't think anybody was being murdered in the other room."

Try as I might, I can't find too much humour in Nathan's joke.

But I manage to put on a wry smile.

"I'll keep it in mind," I say.

Nathan gives me another smile, and then, almost as if I was some sort of sensei, he bows his head. If he wishes me a Good night, then I don't quite hear it.

He brings the door shut behind him.

For about a minute or so, I stare hard at the closed door.

I come to the realisation that nobody else is going to be knocking on my door, that Mark won't even be by to give me a kiss Good night. That tells me that he's taking my need for privacy seriously . . . I guess that he's been in familiar positions in the past—notably when his wife died.

I suppose that, from his own experience, he knows what I need.

I turn my attention back to Lizzie. I give her another stroke, and then tuck myself in beneath the blankets, feeling the gentle warmth of the house on all sides.

But, no matter how hard I try to will myself away to sleep— to slip away into Dreamland—I can't.

Chapter Fifteen

I T MUST BE into the early hours of the morning when I
finally give up on trying to fall asleep. I turn my mind to
whether or not Mark might have some kind of sleeping tablets in
the house. I suppose that, following his wife's death, he was given
all sorts of uppers and downers to help him through the grieving
process.

I help myself out from beneath my blankets, and click on the
light. I only disturb Lizzie so much that she gives a half-annoyed
brurr in my direction. My mind flips through all the eventualities.

That I get caught stalking about Mark's bathroom, in the
middle of the night, fishing through the medicine cabinet . . .
that just won't look *good* . . .

After stalking back and forth behind my bedroom door,
thinking things over, I eventually find myself sitting back down
on the edge of my bed.

Maybe it'd be better just to sit the night out—who *cares* if I
don't manage to get enough sleep?—I can deal with the fallout

tomorrow, ask Mark in a *sane* way if he has anything that might help me to sleep. I'm sure he'd understand my trauma better if I sat him down and *communicated* with him. That's what my therapist Julie used to say, anyway.

I only manage to sit myself down on the edge of my bed for about a minute or so before I'm back up on my feet and stalking about.

Restless.

All of a sudden, the bedroom seems like a prison, as if the walls are pressing in on me from all sides. I turn my attention back to the picture on the wall, of the hillside and sheep, and then down to the bookshelf below, packed almost to bursting with books: all of them, at least from a cursory glance, seeming to deal with various aspects of carpentry.

It's then that the hare-brained idea strikes me.

One of those ones which causes *Problems*, with a capital *P*.

I think back on the conversation I had earlier that evening, with the stuffy gentleman from the insurance firm. About how my claim has—*already*—hit the rocks.

With a slight smile, I admit to myself that I'm *glad* not to have loaned AA any money. That—in the rage of storming out on him—I didn't even pay the nights we'd stayed there.

I find myself sincerely hoping that AA got a really rough time.

As far as I know, they called in the police when he failed to pay the bill.

That'd be the start of some justice.

Some long-awaited justice.

I think about the claim, about my burned-down house.

All things being equal, I probably have enough money to get by for the time being.

Probably even enough to buy another house outright . . . I *will* need a job, though.

I guess that's the rub of the thing.

So what is it that's bothering me?

After all, it was only a house . . . a place where I used to slump down and sleep *occasionally*.

In the end, I reach the conclusion that all this insomnia—all this stalking back and forth about Mark's spare room—has to do with needing some form of closure.

That I actually need to go there—to what remains of my house—and *be* around it.

Alone.

And I suppose that it's this last fact which tips me over the edge.

I dig through my plastic bags, eventually getting together an outfit which is for the most part all black. With that done, I pull on an Army-surplus jacket about my shoulders—black camo—and I slip out through my bedroom door, leaving Lizzie behind to sleep away the rest of the night.

When I get to the top of the staircase, I hear, clear as a bell, a searing, high-pitched scream.

Nathan's scream.

My heart hangs in my throat.

I glance back over my shoulder.

And then, one by one, I prowl down the stairs, heading for the front door.

Chapter Sixteen

I REACH MY HOUSE in about twenty minutes, flagging a stray cab passing by on the main road. The cabbie is an Indian gentleman, with a turban, and he politely asks my destination before driving me where I tell him.

I give him a generous tip, and ask if he can wait for me.

He agrees, and, when I glance back at his taxi, I see that he's produced a newspaper from somewhere, and that he's reading it over with his tired—*but determined*—eyes.

I'm certain that I can still smell the ash in the air; can still feel the prickle of the soot settling on my skin. When I breathe in, the air feels warm—the sensation seems at odds with the way my breath forms before my eyes as steam.

Or how my whole body shudders with every slight stirring of the freezing breeze.

The curtains are drawn on all the houses on the street.

A couple of cats—surely Lizzie's ex-rivals—are huddled up on garden walls, their eyes glassy slivers reflecting the orange streetlights.

Even though I know what to expect, realise *exactly* the reason that I've come back here, it's still a shock. Before me, I make out my neighbour's house—the neighbour I never spoke to—and then, on the other side, Mrs Pietersen's house.

In the middle, there's only a burned-out shell.

The remnants of my home.

Neither of the neighbours' houses have lights lit in their porch areas, and, having lived here for many years, I suppose that the reason must be that they're not in. Both houses, no matter what time of night I would arrive home, would—almost without exception—have their porch lights lit . . . to ward off burglars, or so goes the theory.

I know for a fact that Mrs Pietersen has gone away to stay elsewhere while the necessary structural checks are done, and I suppose that my other neighbour has done something similar.

It means I won't be disturbed as I make my peace.

Good.

I wonder if either of them have been told about the cause of the fire—that it was brought on by a malfunctioning explosive device. I don't suppose that's the sort of detail which the police like to throw around willy-nilly.

As I approach my decimated house, I notice how the front garden has been rendered something of a muddy pit. Although the grass, at this stage of the year, getting on for winter, doesn't look its best by any means, its demise has been exacerbated by the trudge of several dozen firemen. I can still make out their boot prints in the mud.

I approach my front door, and the stainless-steel sheet which covers it—keeping out squatters, I suppose.

The windows, too, all have the same steel sheets over them.

It has the effect of making the place seem deeply unpleasant: *uninviting.* I decide that the sensible way in is around the side alley, and into the back garden.

So that's what I do.

The gate around the side is surprisingly still intact, though I suppose, being steel—or whatever metal it's made of—there's really limited scope for it to melt down into nothing.

It's somewhat strange to see that my back garden is in pretty much the same condition as when I last saw it—when I performed my cat-saving heroics.

As the sole of my trainers treads across the paving slabs, I almost trip over a broken one—a slab which, I suppose, was broken during the fire-fighting efforts. When I draw my foot back upwards, the broken slab makes a blood-curdling *scrape* of concrete on concrete.

I turn to see that the French doors have also been covered with the steel sheets.

The police, or fire brigade, whoever put up these sheets, have been extremely thorough.

However, when I approach one of the steel sheets covering up the French doors, I feel a sort of curiosity throb through me. And I can't help but reach out. To feel the steel sheet. And when I do, when my fingers make contact with the surface, I feel the harsh chill. It seems almost to freeze my blood, to jig my heart up into my throat.

I can't quite say what I expected.

It's not like it's the warmest of nights.

I cling onto the metal, my fingertips working their way to the edge.

Something doesn't feel right.

I give the steel sheet a slight jab.

It gives a little.

And I realise that it's *loose.*

I glance back over my shoulder, afraid that there might be some gossipy neighbour watching on in the early hours of Monday morning. I remind myself of how ridiculous I'm being about breaking into *my own* home.

Then again, I could do without a police car showing up.

Most likely, they'll have all sorts of questions for me . . . about why I haven't been answering my phone to their calls; why I haven't been available to give them information.

And, truth be told, I really have no satisfactory answer to those questions.

Convinced that I'm alone, I pry back the steel sheet covering the French doors, bring it back far enough so that I can peer into the house beyond, into the darkness.

I scold myself for not having had the presence of mind to bring a torch.

Sometimes I really am scatter-brained about these things.

When I go sneaking about at night.

As I think long and hard about peeling the steel sheet back the whole way, somebody speaks to me, from over my shoulder.

"It's okay," the voice says. "They didn't find anything I cleared it out before the fire."

I turn around.

Gaze into the darkness.

Make out the silhouette there—having emerged from a bush's shadow.

But I only recognise who it is when they take a few steps forwards.

When their face comes clear in the streetlight and the moon.

Tabby.

Chapter Seventeen

I N THE DIM LIGHT, I take in Tabby's red hair—which looks black in the darkness.

And then her youthful features.

Her skin has a sheen to it, even in the moonlight.

Like me, she wears all black.

And I know that she's done her very best to avoid detection.

A slight scent of basil drifts through the air when Tabby moves her lips. "Anna," she says, "it's okay, they didn't find any of the guns, anything that would've seemed suspicious. I took care of it."

A creeping numbness seems to have settled in over the surface of my skin. As if I simply can't believe the *nerve* of this woman— this woman, *here*, who worked with AA to burn down my house.

I bring my arm back to smash her in the cheek, but—before I know it—as my arm lingers up, in the air, above my head, at its highest point, a solid grip takes hold.

Prevents me bringing it down.

I struggle for a few moments, before realising that it's in vain.

And I hear another familiar voice, this time coming from behind me.

"Cool it, Anna."

AA.

That only serves to enrage me further, though. Before I can stop myself, I'm gnashing my teeth at Tabby, still standing before me.

AA's hold is sure, and he keeps me from lurching forwards.

"Please, Anna," Tabby says, "you need to listen to us."

"Listen to *you?*" I say. "What for? I don't want anything to do with you people—not anymore. In case you didn't get the memo—I'm *out.*"

I sense that AA's hold on my arm lessens.

I take my chance.

Squirm free from his grip.

Swing my elbow back—catching him in the stomach.

I hear AA puff out air and double over himself.

I turn to Tabby, aim that long-awaited punch . . . but something stops me.

Tabby makes no move to avoid me.

She stands stock-still.

Apparently unafraid.

Communicates it as clearly as if she'd mouthed, *Hit me, Anna. I can take it.*

I wait for AA to seize hold of me again, but he makes no other move to touch me.

Slowly, feeling the adrenalin eke out of my system, I lower my fist to my side.

Leave it there; where it hangs.

Over in one of the hedges, about the circumference of my

garden fence, I hear something stirring. A rabbit? A hedgehog? . . . *Somebody else?*

A chilly wind blows in across the garden and I fold my arms; try to bring some warmth to my blood.

I'm all too aware that both Tabby and AA are staring at me, leaving me in centre stage, waiting to see what I'm going to do next. I suppose I should take it as something of a compliment that I'm not *that* predictable . . . seeing as they already knew to lurk about my house, apparently knowing that I'd return at some point.

"What's this about?" I say, finally shattering the silence. "What've you *possibly* got to tell me?"

"We didn't do it," Tabby says, not moving an inch from her spot.

"What're you talking about?" I say, shifting a glance back over my shoulder, at AA, and thinking—with some joy—about how he *really does* look like shit.

I wonder if he's been turfed out of the hotel yet.

"The fire," Tabby says. "We didn't set it."

I screw up my forehead, thinking about the hotel room, and AA's reaction—how he said nothing to deny his involvement with my house fire.

How he effectively confirmed that he knew all about it.

"Then," I say, not quite believing my ears, "who did?"

Tabby shifts a glance over my shoulder, to AA standing behind me.

I wonder if Tabby and AA are armed because, if they are, it puts me at a distinct *disadvantage.*

Tabby breathes out hot air, making it form a cloud in front of her face. "It's a long story, Anna, and it's early in the morning; only a little above freezing—can we arrange to speak later?"

"No," I say, quite decided on the fact. "Tell me now, or I'm leaving."

There's a long pause.

I look around, look to the silent, sleeping houses.

Not a light lit in visual range.

But that doesn't mean nobody's watching.

The moonlight catches Tabby's green eyes, and, for a second, they seem to be clear; glistening like a pair of marbles. "We've been tracking Brian's movements," she says.

I roll my eyes, then give an exasperated shake of the head. "*Why?*"

"Because," Tabby says, "we don't believe that he was entirely truthful about leaving us all to it—about giving us a fresh start. About him *respecting* us enough to let us loose." She meets AA's eye again, then says, "I think the whole bomb-in-your-house thing only goes to prove that."

I glance back at AA—see that he wears a stern expression.

That he could really do with a haircut.

Not to mention a shave.

"Yeah," I say, turning back to Tabby, "and what's your proof that Brian set the bomb in my house—why should I believe that it wasn't you and AA?"

Tabby looks away from me. Her tongue makes a rounded lump in her cheek, as if she's searching for some expression. Finally, she says, "They've been trying to get shot of you, Anna —*Brian has*—ever since you got back."

Again, I screw up my eyes, look from Tabby to AA. "Look," I say, to AA, "do you think you could come stand round here where I can see you? It's making me nervous having you standing right behind me, breathing down my neck."

AA meets my eye for a moment, and then he acquiesces.

He goes to stand beside Tabby so that the two of them are in front of me now.

That *does* feel better.

Though I can't quite say for certain that I won't still want to kill one—or *both*—of them before the night's over.

"Only," Tabby continues, "Brian set it up so that Charlie Branwick would take care of you—so that one of his hoods would take care of you."

"And?" I say, looking to AA. "Why didn't you tell me this earlier?"

AA gives me a slight smile, but it soon dissolves from his lips when he sees that I'm not yet ready to reciprocate. "Because I believed you when I said you wanted out of this—that you didn't want to hear another word about Brian Mathewson."

"Yeah," I say, feeling a touch exasperated now, "but it would've been nice to know that there was a hit out on me."

AA shakes his head. "We thought we'd got it all tied up, Amy—"

"*Amy?*" I say, unable to stop butting in. "You mean Charlie-Branwick's-daughter *Amy?*"

AA nods.

Amy—the last I saw of her—as with Tabby and AA, was headed in a completely separate direction. But, then again, it seems that I was a little naïve to think that the others could keep themselves apart. That they'd *honour* what we'd agreed.

I turn back to AA. "You're all working together? The three of you?"

Tabby and AA exchange glances.

Neither of them says anything, but their guilty expressions speak volumes.

I look away, then shake my head in the direction of the fence, at the neighbouring garden. "Jesus," I say. "Anything else I need to know?"

"Like I was saying," AA says, "Amy managed to get through to the guy who was set on your case, and she was able to get some money through to him—able to pay him off for the time being." He gives another uneasy smile. "It's not easy to buy off an assassin, and me and Tabby knew that we'd have to take care of him eventually . . . it was just to bide time."

I give a shake of my head, then look AA back in the eye. "The debt?" I say. "That was why you wanted money from me—you were paying off the assassin?"

AA gives a glum nod by way of reply.

I stand there, in my back garden, behind my burned-down house, trying to get my brain around all these tangled strands Tabby and AA have—*apparently*—been weaving around my naïve, newly peaceful little life.

And there I was, thinking that I'd escaped.

That I'd got away at last.

Guess that just goes to prove how naïve I really am.

Just as I'm on the point of drawing a line under this whole episode, telling Tabby and AA to just get lost, I snap to my senses. See something in what they've been telling me that makes no sense.

I shoot AA and Tabby with a glare. "If you knew that they were going to burn down my house, if they were going to try to kill me, then why didn't you do something to stop them—why didn't you think to tell me before?"

Both Tabby and AA stare back at me.

In the end, AA slips Tabby a sidelong glance, and says, "I think you'd better take this one."

———

Tabby goes on to outline the exact extent of their surveillance of Brian Mathewson and, in particular, his attempts to take care of me for good. She details out how Amy is still within her father—Charlie Branwick's—inner circle.

Charlie Branwick, apparently, doesn't yet realise that she was the one responsible for the death of Grendelin, back on that anonymous Caribbean island Brian Mathewson flew us all to.

Or, if Charlie Branwick *does* realise that his daughter brought about her death, then perhaps he believes that it was only forthcoming.

I don't prod at the intricacies of the thing.

Sometimes not knowing information can be just as powerful as knowing it; and I certainly have no idea what the extent of my involvement with all this is actually going to be.

As the winter air cuts through our hunched-over forms, all of us standing about in my back garden, Tabby goes on to say, "The bribes—the money AA was paying out to keep the hood from following through with the hit . . . it dried up, and the hood claimed that there was nothing to be done. That he was going to have to go through with the thing. So AA got hold of money from . . . *somewhere else* . . ."

I glance to AA.

His eyes avoid mine.

I turn back to Tabby. "And where'd he get it from?"

"We'll get to that," Tabby replies, rapid-fire. "It's not important right now."

"But AA said that he was going to be in deep 'doo-doo' if he didn't manage to repay it as soon as possible, and, well, from what you say about him getting hold of that money to save my skin; it makes me feel just a touch *guilty* . . . but, then again, I had no way of knowing." I give a shrug. "Who knows, if I *had* known maybe I would've taken matters into my own hands—managed to see off that hood whenever he showed up to murder me."

Tabby shakes her head. "Oh, Anna," she says, "you really don't get it."

"Don't get *what?*" I say, anger creeping into my voice now— merited anger, you might say, given how I've been kept in the dark here.

"Even if we could've kept up the payments to the assassin, they would've eventually cottoned on, and sent someone else," she says. "That defective *bomb*, the one which they set in your house, that was their way of telling you to take care."

"Yeah," I say, "it wasn't exactly subtle."

A smile tweaks AA's lips. "And when have you *ever* known Brian to be subtle?"

There's a pregnant pause in the conversation while that particular observation is allowed to mature and grow between us.

"We couldn't *do* anything, Anna," Tabby says, "otherwise they would've known that we were watching—they would know that there's a leak within their operation; and, well, it seems fairly obvious that all indications will point to Amy . . . and we don't want her to get into danger either."

"So my house was collateral damage?" I say.

AA sniffs a laugh. "Look, Anna, if we'd really wanted you dead then we could've just chosen not to tell you at all."

I glare back at AA, wiping that smirk right off his lips. "Or you could've just told me the truth from the start and not skulked about in the shadows playing God."

AA stays quiet when I say that.

"Anyway," I say, with a slight smile, "you must have wanted

that house to go up as much as they did . . . with the memory stick on the premises, and all—your details are on it too, it would surely have been destroyed. And you two would be absolved." I look to AA. "The first thing *he* asked me was if I had the memory stick . . . it would've been nice and convenient for it to be destroyed."

Tabby shakes her head. "No," she says, "you're wrong about that, Anna. That memory stick is the one thing which we have over Brian—why he gave it to us, I still don't understand. But that memory stick needs to remain safe whatever the cost." She pauses for a moment and then adds, "You *have* put it somewhere safe, haven't you?"

I think back to the bookshelf in Mark's house—where I stashed the Death Log.

And that gets me thinking about other things . . .

I look back around my garden, take in the familiar silhouettes of my bushes, the trees sprouting up from the ground. Everything which I once believed to belong to me and—by some stupid extension of thinking—to be on some level untouchable.

When I turn to Tabby and AA again, I say, "I'm putting others in danger, aren't I?"

"What'd you mean?" Tabby says.

"If I'm around them—I'm being followed. I have to take care with who I speak to, who I'm seen with." I pause for a long moment. "Where I'm *staying*."

Tabby shifts a glance at AA, then looks back at me.

Finally, she gives a doleful nod.

Chapter Eighteen

MY HEART RAPS hard against my ribcage as I climb the stairs of Mark's home.

It's nearly three o'clock in the morning, and I feel somewhat like an adolescent who's been out on the town, and who is only now sneaking in.

The air still smells of the wonderful spices Mark used to cook dinner with earlier on, and the central heating is certainly welcome. Being thrifty myself, I tend to flip the heating off in the early hours, but I suppose—from Mark's financial state—he really has little reason to be thrifty. He can afford to throw about the odd bundle of notes; here and there.

It's only when I reach the top step that I think I've managed to do it—that I've managed to burgle my way into Mark's house with little fanfare.

And then, with a gentle *creak* as my foot weighs down a loosened floorboard, I turn to see Mark's bedroom door opening.

He appears in the darkened gap, silhouetted by the moonlight shining in through his bedroom skylight. He is shirtless—naked except for his pyjama bottoms—and rubbing the sleep out of his eyes.

Finally he looks to me through dopey eyes, squints hard. "Anna?" he says, his voice a husky whisper. "Is that you?"

I've always wondered how I might answer a question like this in real life . . . and I guess that, now, I get to see.

"Yes," I say, whispering in reply, "it's me, I was just . . ." and then I allow my words to float away, as if that'll be explanation enough, as if Mark will be able to fill in the gaps for himself.

Mark blinks a couple of times. He leans his bare shoulder up against the doorframe, crosses his arms over his chest. He mushes his lips together as if doing some sort of warm-up before attempting to speak. "Thought you were Nathan," he says. "Sometimes he, uh . . . sleepwalks."

"Yes," I say, "he came into my room—told me earlier." I pause for a beat, then add, "About the night *terrors*."

Mark nods to himself, as if this was some sort of acknowledged truth . . . then again, I suppose that it is—in a way.

His eyelids droop down, as if he's about to fall asleep right where he stands.

I smile back at him. "Go on," I say, "I won't keep you."

Realising that now—if I have *any* chance of getting away with my night-time foray—I have to wander off, I turn my back to him. Make towards the guest room. Although I don't feel even the slightest bit tired, I manage to sneak a fake yawn into my response. "See you in the morning."

I've almost reached my bedroom door when Mark speaks to me again. "Anna?" he says.

I feel a tingling sensation pass through my blood.

A chill tickle my spine.

"Yes?" I say, not turning around, my hand now on the guest-room doorknob.

"Would you, uh . . . if you're feeling okay, that is . . ."

Somewhat accustomed to male, verbal clumsiness, I give a slight smile.

Then I turn back.

Go to him.

Chapter Nineteen

I WAKE UP with the sun in my eyes.

When I pat about me—feeling the soft mattress beneath my touch—I recall that I'm in Mark's bed; that I ended up in his bed last night, when I returned.

I have a stale taste in my mouth, just like I always do whenever I wake up. The air, though, smells pleasantly of *man* . . . Mark's distinctive scent: musk mixed up with wood shavings.

Soon enough, I realise that I'm naked beneath the duvet.

I glance to the floor, see that my clothes are all screwed up there.

With no sign of Mark about the bedroom—and the door itself firmly, and snugly shut—I make a grab for my clothes. I've just about managed to haul my vest down over my head and to haul some knickers up over my waist when I hear the door creaking open behind me.

When I turn, I'm surprised to see Nathan standing there.

Wearing his frog-green school uniform—the same one my

own son, Ben, wears to school—he peers in around the doorframe.

The moment that our eyes meet, I can almost *feel* the crackle of discomfort passing through the air.

"Oh," he says, quickly looking away, then backing out. "*Sorry!*"

He brings the door shut with a slam.

I hear his footsteps thudding along the landing outside, and him calling out, "Dad? Dad!"

Poor little bugger, he probably got something of a shock seeing me sitting on the edge of his father's bed . . . although, having said that, I really *do* hope it was a shock—I could do with *not* finding out that Mark's something of a Don Juan.

I pluck up various other pieces of clothing and—eventually—have managed to assemble something of an outfit border-line acceptable for walking about somebody else's house first thing in the morning.

I break free of Mark's bedroom, glance out through the door, decide that Nathan's not going to come walking along any time soon, and I manage to make it back to my bedroom: the guest bedroom.

When I open up the door, I'm immediately greeted with the unmistakable—*pungent*—odour of cat urine. On instinct, I look down, and see Lizzie there, peering up at me, her cat face sketched with concern.

I give her a vague smile. "Sorry," I say. "Should've thought of that before, shouldn't I?"

———

Once I've managed to get my act together, and discovered the extent of Lizzie's urination—not much more than a discoloured patch on a corner of wallpaper—I hoik myself off to the shower, then return to put some clothes on.

I go with a simple, turquoise t-shirt over a pair of black jeans.

In the absence of a full-length mirror, I don't have the option of switching in and out of outfits, searching for Just The Right One. In retrospect, though, that's probably for the best.

With Lizzie bobbing in and out around my feet, I make my way downstairs, and right into the thick smells of butter and eggs cooking.

When I turn my attention to the cook, standing at the kitchen stove, I see that—of course—it's Mark. He stands with his back to me, an apron tied up around his waist. Underneath the apron, he has on an old shirt, frayed about the hem, over a pair of battered jeans—clothes he, clearly, uses for his carpentry.

He senses me enter, and turns to look. He gives me a broad smile. "Up and about?" he says.

"Yeah," I say, blushing a touch, and then taking my place at the kitchen table.

I look about the place, and then say, "Where's Nathan?"

"At school," Mark replies, his focus back on the eggs he's cooking. "Shot out about five minutes ago."

I briefly consider filling Mark in on mine and Nathan's impromptu salutation earlier that morning but, in the end, decide not to cause a stir.

Mark continues, "Sorry if I gave you a shock—not being there when you woke up." There's a *sizzle* from the pan as he stirs in some more butter. "It's just that I like to get an early start on the day—to get down to my workshop while I can."

"That's fine," I say, with a smile.

Mark finishes up cooking the eggs—*scrambled*—and deposits

them over two slices of buttered toast. I notice, too, that he has a pot of coffee steaming away. He sets about pouring out a pair of cups.

He brings everything over to the table and it only enters my mind that I should—you know—maybe offer him my assistance with *something* after he's already dished everything up and we're sitting opposite one another.

We eat our respective breakfasts in silence: me—*lady I am*—finishing before Mark does, and then sitting back to sip on the delicious, rich-tasting coffee that he's prepared.

When Mark swallows his final mouthful, and sets his cutlery neatly down on his plate, he picks up his own cup of coffee, takes the slightest of sips, wincing slightly either at the bitterness or at the heat. He sets his cup back down then glances across the table at me. "How're you doing, Anna?" he says.

"Fine," I say, trying my best to smile pleasantly in reply —*neutrally*—to make it seem like what I say really is true.

Mark nods back at me.

Takes another swig of coffee.

Sets the cup back down again.

"It's just," Mark says, "last night, you know . . ."

I feel my chest tighten, thinking that he's going to bring up how I snuck out of his house.

. . . And then back *in* again.

"Well"—Mark gives a slight smile, stares down into his coffee cup—"I didn't want to seem demanding, or anything, didn't want you to feel like . . . you know . . ."

"Like I was *compelled* to sleep with the master of the house in exchange for room and board?"

Mark smiles widely, then gives a shake of his head. "Yeah," he says, a slight chuckle in his voice, "something like that."

"In that case," I reply, "there's no need to be worried." I pause for a second, taking another sip of my own coffee, then add, "I was *quite* willing."

By the time we've finished up our breakfast, and I've helped Mark to slot the plates into the dishwasher, I can't help feeling that I could quite easily get used to this domestic situation. And it's only, really, when I'm through with cleaning my teeth—when I've cleared up Lizzie's mess in the guest room—and when I'm lying back on my freshly made bed that I realise that this can't last.

That every second I spend in Mark's house, it's another that I bring him into danger.

Extreme danger.

Chapter Twenty

DESPITE MY RESOLUTION—*my decision*—that I simply can't stay any longer in Mark's house, I decide not to tell him until later on that evening.

I need a little time to work out my plan.

The first one I call up is AA.

Between the two of us, we work out a time for him to come and pick me up; a little after nine in the evening. It's good to have a deadline. It means that I won't be able to back out. That there'll be someone else depending on me going through with what I've already promised.

When I question him further about this money he needs *urgently* so that he can pay back . . . whoever it is that he needs to *pay back* . . . he gets elusive.

I can't quite shake the feeling that what was once urgent isn't so any longer.

I wonder if he's managed to source funds from elsewhere; or

if he and Tabby—God knows Amy *too*—have come to some other agreeable solution.

When I ask if I can have contact details for Tabby and Amy —seeing as it appears that I won't be able to avoid them, for my sins—AA again gets elusive, claiming that we can talk *all about it* later on that evening.

When he picks me up.

AA hangs up on me, and it leaves me to tell Mark that I won't be staying.

Easy . . . yeah, right . . .

Mark disappears throughout the course of the day, only appearing at lunch to 'throw together' the most delicious ham sandwich I've ever tasted and then at mid-afternoon to make another brew of coffee. Each time he does emerge, though, I can't help but feel myself becoming lost in the thick, sawdust smell which clings to him . . . which seems so *familiar* and so *warm* . . . and it makes it all the harder to realise the truth.

That I *can't* stay.

When Nathan arrives back from school, he greets both me and Mark in the kitchen, the two of us already setting about making dinner.

Tonight's dinner will be lasagne.

I spoon together the sauce, melting cheese, smelling the garlic and onions waft about in the air, under Mark's watchful—*but benev-olent*—gaze. And it's then that I decide to break the news. It's just as he reaches around me, brings the wooden spoon up to his mouth so that he might give it a cursory lick, that I judge the time's right.

"Mark?" I say.

"Hmm?" he says, his tongue still mostly busy tasting the sauce.

"What would you say if I had to head off someplace else?"

" 'Someplace else' ?" he says, in a level tone of voice, betraying no surprise at all. And then, glancing down at the cheese sauce I'm stirring, "Chuck in a dash of salt."

I do as he says, aware of him buzzing about busily behind me, looking through cupboards, sweeping through several drawers. I keep up the conversation. "It's just," I say, "I think I'm going to have to take off." I pause for a second, realising that I'm allowing the sauce to stick to the bottom of the pan. I give it a couple of vigorous scrapes then add, "*Tonight.*"

Mark doesn't answer right away, and when I turn around, I see that he's crouched down, and digging through a cupboard. Finally, he straightens up with a transparent, oven-safe dish in his hands. He gives me an unconvincing smile. "Gonna need this," he says, and then plonks it down on the kitchen counter.

Apparently considering my question, he scratches at the back of his neck, and then turns to me, says, "Oh, that's fine, I mean, whenever you need to come and go"—he flashes a wide, and even more unconvincing, smile—"feel free to use the house as a base."

I feel my pulse pounding in my temples.

I tell myself that I need to keep on going—that I can't possibly leave things *here*. "That's great," I say, although my voice sounds dry, unfeeling almost. "There was something else I wanted to ask you."

"*What?*" Mark says, this time sounding short.

The first time that I've ever heard anything approaching anger enter his voice.

It knocks me back a touch.

I turn to him, see that he's now busying himself with buttering the oven-safe dish.

He gets down low on the kitchen counter, as I picture he must be whenever he's sanding the edges of some wooden object.

"I was wondering," I say, trying not to sound taken aback, "if you wouldn't mind me leaving Lizzie here." I feel something stick in my throat, feeling the pressure in the air between us now . . . almost palpable. "I'll be back in a few days."

Mark straightens up suddenly from his buttering of the dish. He brushes his hands together as if he might be getting himself shot of some sawdust. "*Fine*," he replies.

We go on cooking.

I have no idea what to say to him next.

As I continue to stir away at the lasagne sauce, Nathan wanders in. He hovers about for a while, roots around in a cupboard and then grabs hold of a few breadsticks. Apparently noting the fraught tension in the kitchen, he departs and—from the sitting room—I hear the TV coming to life.

"Anna?" Mark says.

It surprises me to hear Mark speak again . . . I thought that he might be giving me the silent treatment.

Again, I feel my skin all prickle into goose pimples.

I risk a sidelong glance at him, and am surprised to note that he stares right back at me.

"What do you do?" he says.

I feel that question echo about my brain, and yet I can't quite see myself spitting out an answer. For some reason, staring into Mark's hazel eyes strips all words from the surface of my tongue.

Mark turns back to chopping up some tomatoes. He looks just a *shade* menacing to be wielding that extremely large— extremely *sharp*—knife of his. "It's a simple question," he says, and then looks to me. "And a simple answer."

I think back to our earlier dates, and when, on some sort of whim, I told him *exactly* what I did . . . what I am . . . what I *was* . . . and he did little more than laugh at me.

What does he expect from me now?

Does he expect me to say that I'm a travelling salesperson?

An insurance broker?

. . . Though that'd probably help out quite a bit in my current circumstances, or might've helped me *not* to get backed into the position which I now find myself in.

But looking back into those hazel eyes, I know that he just wants *an* answer . . . just something to go on.

When I speak, my throat feels impossibly dry. And I can't quite get over the fear that I won't be able to get any comprehensible words out at all. ". . . I *kill* . . ." I manage to utter.

And then the phone starts to ring.

Chapter Twenty-One

ALTHOUGH I WANT to see Mark's reaction, he strides off in the direction of the ringing phone.

And I can't tell whether or not he heard me at all.

As I busy myself with chopping up some carrot—picking up the slack which Mark left to me—I realise I can hardly smell the thick, cheesy scents wafting up from the saucepans. The delicious meal that we're preparing together.

For any other—*normal*—woman this would be like some kind of scene from paradise. A man who knows how to cook, who's good with his *hands*, and who wants to spend time with her . . . but, as I found out a long time ago, I'm not a normal woman.

While Mark speaks on the phone, I feel Lizzie wrap herself about my legs, purring her head off. It's no wonder that she's decided to show her face—no doubt she's smelled out the cheese and is *extremely* curious. Lizzie is something of a cheese maniac.

Although I know that the vet would probably scold me for doing so, I drop a chunk of cheese on the floor.

Lizzie pounces on it as nimbly as she might a field mouse.

Just like that—*a click of the fingers*—the chunk of cheese is gone.

I turn my attention back to the cooking.

I can't avoid overhearing Mark, over my shoulder, speaking on the phone.

". . . What? . . . But that's ridiculous . . . What'd you mean? . . . The paperwork says nothing of the sort! . . . Sure I can go and dig out a copy but I'm in the middle of dinner . . . Yes, call me back . . . Uh-huh . . . *Fine.*"

I feel a shift in his barely repressed anger, and that it's now being directed at the other end of the telephone, whoever might be on it.

He hangs the phone up and the base unit gives a satisfied *twee-twah.*

When Mark arrives back to the chopping board, where he was busy with the tomatoes, he goes about his work without a word to me.

After we've been standing there in silence for the longest time, I finally pluck up the courage to ask, "Who was it?"

Mark glances to me. He blinks a couple of times. And his mood seems to clear. He gives a shake of his head, even a slight smile. "Oh, nothing . . . just been bothering me all day, that's all."

Although I'm ready to allow the matter to drop—not really in any state of mind to want to stoke the embers of Mark's anger again—he carries on without my intervention.

"It's Nathan's biological father," Mark says. "He wants visitation rights."

I breathe in the gentle scent of cooking olive oil and butter—garlic and onions sizzling away—and it feels almost as if those smells are dealing me a delicious full-body massage.

"About earlier," Mark says, laying the knife back down on the counter, alongside the chopped-up tomatoes, "I'm sorry—I didn't want to seem impertinent. It's just that this has been on my mind all day; haven't been able to think clearly." He gives me another gentle smile. "Your job, it's not important. Whatever it is."

And although I feel as if everything within me is screaming out for me to clarify with him that—*really*—I do kill for a living, Mark flaps his hand as if waving away the mere idea of me spelling it out to him . . . one more time.

Shaking his head, Mark takes up the knife again, slices up the last of the tomatoes. "Sometimes I forget, working from home, that other people have to actually leave the house to go and earn money."

I have nothing at all to say to that.

Mark brushes off the last of the tomatoes, depositing them into the saucepan. Then he turns to me, gives me a warm smile, then reaches out and lays his hand on my shoulder. "And what I said, about this being your base, I mean it—I'll keep your stuff safe"—Lizzie rubs her head up against Mark's leg, and he scoops her up in his arms—"and I'll keep this little lady safe, too."

Lizzie purrs away in Mark's arms.

An unashamed flirt.

———

We get through dinner, and it's incredibly delicious.

Throughout, I can't help but feel just a touch jealous observing the interactions between Nathan and Mark—seeing how Nathan, instinctively, looks to Mark for approval after having said something to me, or if he goes on about some incident at school that day.

It makes my stomach itch to think that the Powers That Be are attempting to break up this happy family dynamic. I wonder if Mark's wife's death, about two years ago, has something to do with this renewed interest. Perhaps they want to shuttle Nathan to another—more 'standard'—mother-father family unit.

I don't really understand how these things work.

For dessert, Mark heats up some chocolate pudding in the microwave, and I lose myself to the chocolatey mess. It makes everything else go away for those short moments, right until the second when I lick the final chocolate drop clean from the spoon.

Then the phone starts ringing again.

Mark—visibly containing his irritation—collects up our plates, then sends Nathan on his way, back to the sitting room, to watch TV, scruffing up his hair as he leaves the table.

I offer to clean the pots and slot the dishes into the dish-washer while Mark sees to the phone. In my peripheral vision, I observe him slinking his way out of the kitchen and off in the direction of what I assume to be his study.

Already, with the phone glued to the side of his head, Mark mumbles all sorts to the person on the other end, about being on his way to fetch the paperwork *right now.*

I surprise even myself with my efficiency in getting the plates all done, all slotted into the dishwasher. When I'm finished with my tidying away, I head upstairs, to the guest room.

On the way there, though, I think to poke my head into the sitting room.

On the turtle-green—*well-loved*—sofa, I see Nathan lying flat, the top of his head facing me.

I spy Lizzie lying on his stomach; see Nathan's hand disap-pearing into her fur.

Lizzie's purrs carry all the way to the doorway.

And neither one of them sees me as I slip away.

Leaving them to it.

———

With everything ready, I check my phone and see that the time has just ticked over to nine p.m. Sure enough—if nothing else a stickler for punctuality—I see that AA's all pulled up outside the house, his canary-yellow car puttering exhaust up into the winter air.

I can just about make out his silhouette within.

His hands grasping the steering wheel as he faces forwards.

I dash through the house, glance to the bookshelf, thinking about the memory stick—about the Death Log—and then decide that it's for the best to leave it here.

Where it *won't* be on my person.

I have no idea where AA will be taking me.

. . . I have no idea—*really*—if AA, let alone Tabby, are to be trusted.

This could all just be a ruse to get their hands on the Death Log.

And to finish with me.

I wonder whether it was such a good idea to give AA Mark's address . . . now he knows where my boyfriend, and his adopted son, live . . .

But I try not to let it bother me.

There's nothing I can do about it now.

I've transferred the essentials I'm taking away with me into one of the plastic bags. I'm going to look like a bag lady striding up to AA's car. I now wear the denim jacket over my turquoise top and jeans. Probably not the right kit to go mountaineering in, but hopefully mountaineering's not on the cards.

I pad down the stairs just as Mark—a face like thunder—emerges from the study, the phone gripped down tightly at his side as if it was an axe. When he meets my eye, his expression softens. He gives me a smile. "All set, then?" he says.

I nod back at him, still standing in the middle of the staircase. "Think so."

Mark jerks a thumb over his shoulder. "That your ride—waiting on the curb?"

"AA," I say, "yes."

Again, I think about what Mark must think of AA . . . and his suspicions surrounding my connection to him.

But I have hardly a second to *really* get down into depth about that because, before I know it, there's a *buzz* at the door.

Both me and Mark turn to look, as if we're both totally stumped at what this might signify.

Before I get a chance to tell Mark that I'll get it, he treads over to the door, notches down the latch and opens up.

There, clear as day, stands AA.

Tonight, he wears a silvery grey suit with a neat, cream shirt; three buttons undone. I catch a puff of pineapple wafting in with him . . . one of AA's *newer* fragrances, I suppose.

AA gives me a nod of acknowledgement over Mark's shoulder, and then turns his attention to Mark himself, pumping his hand. "Adam," AA says to Mark. "Adam Alderknot. Pleased to meet you."

Bemused, Mark glances back at me.

AA turns to look at me. "Thought I'd give you a hand with your bags, but"—his gaze lingers over the single plastic bag which dangles from my fingertips—"it looks like you've packed light."

"That's okay," I say, taking the final few steps down into the hallway.

Side stepping Mark, I thrust my plastic bag into AA's chest.

AA takes it from me, puffing out his cheeks and staggering as he does so.

I turn my glare onto him, then say, "Meet you in the car, okay?"

AA nods to Mark. "Nice to meet you," he says, and then ventures back out into the night, back to the waiting car.

Mark looks out after AA—to the road. "That's some car," he says. "A pretty decent motor."

Mark himself has what is probably known in snobby circles as a Dad Estate: one of those rectangular-shaped, practical cars; all the very latest in safety design; child locks on the back doors . . . probably bulletproof too.

Mark looks back to me.

And it's then that I feel I *have* to say something. "This looks bad, doesn't it?" I say. "I mean, this *strange*, well-dressed man showing up at nine o'clock at night to whisk me away?"

Mark gives me that same warm smile of his . . . the one which is threatening to cause me to fall in love with him—if I don't watch myself. "Nah," he says, and sounds as though he means it. "I suppose that these sorts of quirks are all becoming of the professional assassin."

I feel my stomach twist around the lasagne.

I swallow hard.

"Yeah, I mean . . ." I just about get out before Mark cuts me off.

"Look, Anna," Mark says, his smile fading a little, but none of the sparkle going out of his eyes, "I know what a tall order this is—you know—moving in, being with me and Nathan, it's a big move, and, maybe, if circumstances had been different we could've done things differently; we could've taken things more slowly."

He breathes in, takes the breath right to the pit of his lungs. "I'm a realist, I know that it's a big undertaking, but I trust you." He smiles again. "Just as I hope you trust me."

It's then that I can't stop myself.

My whole body just lurches forwards.

And I press my lips—*hard*—against his.

Hoping this won't be the last time I see him alive.

Chapter Twenty-Two

"WHERE'RE WE GOING?" I say to AA, after ten minutes' driving.

I feel the car engine trundling hard through the seat.

The air smells as if it has recently been disinfected—*rigorously*—and I suppose that AA's been turning things around since he was sleeping in his car.

I can still taste the lasagne all over my tongue, and would give just about anything to turn around and go and have seconds.

With Mr Perfect.

But I know that's simply not an option.

The world won't allow me.

AA flips the indicator and a plasticky *tick-tick-tick* sounds from somewhere in the dashboard. "Scotland," AA replies, turning us onto the motorway slip road.

" 'Scotland' ?" I say, realising that maybe, now, in actual fact mountaineering *is* on the cards . . .

AA pulls out onto the motorway, glances back at me, then, with a slight smile, repeats, "*Scotland.*"

We drive on for another minute or so, and I feel myself becoming hypnotised by the constant white lines sweeping beneath the car. Then I ask, "Why Scotland?"

AA gives a Gallic shrug—and a pout to boot. He grips the wheel and stares on out across the approaching road. "You know how Brian feels about Scotland."

"His best friend's from Scotland," I reply, referencing Charlie Branwick—Amy's father.

We drive on without another word to one another.

When AA seems to twig that I've got nothing more to say for myself, he opens up the throttle, bundling us along the motorway, taking us past the—*impossibly slow*—moving traffic. He seems strangely alert, drawn to attention; more so than at any point I've seen him in the past few days.

As AA trundles the car onwards, I feel myself slowly—*but inevitably*—being pulled down into sleep.

———

I wake up feeling a little dampness on my chin.

And a *harsh* chill in the air.

I open my eyes. Glance around. Realise that there's light all around.

Artificial light.

Flooding the car.

No engine sounds.

And no AA, either.

It takes another few panicked moments for me to gather that we're parked up at a service station. I look about the deserted forecourt; that thick, *heady* stench of petrol making its way up my nostrils now.

Finally, my eyes come to rest on the station shop and—beyond the glass—I make out AA standing at the counter, apparently paying for the petrol he's just purchased.

It's in that moment that I think to glance across, to the driver's side of the car. I notice that the keys dangle from the ignition. I know that—*if I really wanted*—I could slip over into the driver's seat, drive away. Never be heard from again.

Never see Mark again.

Never see my own *children* again.

But, maybe, that'd be for the best . . .

Before I have a chance to act on these newly awakened urges, AA slips out of the petrol station shop, looking just as crisp and clean as he did when he arrived on Mark's doorstep—in that silvery suit of his. As he approaches the car, he rubs his hands vigorously together before bringing them up to his mouth and blowing hot air into them.

When he notices that I'm awake, he flashes a smile at me.

He opens up the door, bringing a fresh, frosty draught in with him.

I listen to the car suspension groan as he settles in his seat. He brings the door shut with a slam. The whole car shakes with his actions.

"How's it going, sleepyhead?" he says.

I realise that I'm still slumped up in my seat, and I use my elbow to prop myself back upright. I rub the heels of my hands hard into my eyes, trying to bring myself around. "What time is it?" I ask.

AA turns the ignition and the engine fires long and hard.

In response, hot air floods out through the plastic vents.

For a couple of seconds it's overwhelming.

The difference between the chill and the heat.

But then my body gets used to it.

AA glances through the steering column and to the dash-board. "Just gone one in the morning," he says, and then turns back to me with a wide grin.

I give AA a shake of the head, and squint at him. "How'd you do it?" I say. "How'd you stay awake?"

AA arches an eyebrow and then taps the side of his nose.

A gesture which—*really*—could mean anything and everything.

He pulls us back out onto the motorway, drives along the near-deserted tarmac, illuminated only by the odd set of head-lights; punctuated only by the lorries which trundle along in the slow lane. I only get a brief glimpse of them as AA flies past doing a speed that I don't even have the stomach to confirm with a glance at the dashboard instruments.

"How long till we get there?" I say, feeling a yawn sneak its way across my face, and then rack the rest of my body.

"Oh," AA jiggles his suit sleeve and I realise that he wears a wristwatch too—in addition to having the clock on his dash-board, "I'd say around two, three hours."

"You're making some record time, aren't you?"

AA gives me a sidelong glance, and a mock solemn expres-sion. "Well, I have been driving ridiculously fast," he says, before turning back to the steering wheel.

———

I slip in and out of consciousness for the rest of the journey.

I've never been the best at managing to sleep in cars, and this particular voyage doesn't appear to be proving the exception.

I'm in a half-asleep state when I feel the road surface beneath us change from the steady tarmac it's been all along. I listen to gravel ping off the underside of the car, and listen to it crunch beneath the tyres.

I raise myself back up in my seat and peer out through the windscreen.

To the road ahead.

Nothing more than a narrow, gravel track.

I look to AA, as if confirming just from a glance that this is our destination.

AA only gives me a vague nod.

I only realise that we've reached our destination when, quite suddenly, AA brings the car to a halt. The tyres slide along the loose gravel. And then, without another word, AA swings his arm up and over my backrest, then turns his attention out through the rear window, apparently reversing us into a space.

Once he brings us to a halt, he leaves the engine ticking over for another few seconds, before switching off the ignition. And everything—*all at once*—trundles down into silence.

The only sound comes from the light *tick-tick* of some mechanism within the car's bonnet.

I look to AA. "We're here?" I say.

AA unravels himself from his seatbelt.

When he punches the Release button, the seatbelt whizzes back into its plastic shell, propelled by its spring-loaded mechanism.

"Come on," AA mumbles, over his shoulder, stepping out through the driver's door. "I'll cook you up some breakfast."

———

I'm still somewhat out of it when AA shoves a torch into my chest.

He's at least given a cursory thought to my current state of mind since he's already switched the torch on for me . . . so that I don't need to scale that particular mental hurdle at this time in the morning.

And, to be honest, I'm quite glad about that.

I feel the freezing-cold air nibbling at my face. By my reckoning the temperature is five or six degrees colder than it was down south, in London. Whenever I move my legs, it feels almost as if the air is making the conscious effort to freeze up my muscles.

But even *I* know that the air itself isn't *that* malevolent.

I shine the yellowish circle of the torch up ahead of me—to the building which AA has parked us up outside.

Bricks. A good start.

At least we won't be staying in some ready-to-crumble wooden shack.

Reassuring.

As AA leads us around the side of the building, a torch in his own hand, I think to turn back and look to the car, parked up outside. "Uh," I begin, somewhat unconvincingly, "do you really think it's inconspicuous to leave your car parked up there?"

AA doesn't so much as look back, but I'm *certain* that he somehow finds a way to aim a shrug at me. "Got a tarpaulin—I'll go slip it over the car when I've got you set up inside."

For the remainder of our approach to the house, I button my lip . . . knowing my place when I'm told it.

It's only when we stand on the doorstep—the doorstep to

what seems, at least to me, to be a cottage—that I hear, over off on the horizon the sound of crashing waves. And then, as if by magic, a hint of stale *saltiness* in the air . . . those smells of the sea.

"Are we . . ." I just about get out.

"Yup," AA replies, scrabbling with a tinkling chain of keys, before finally separating one of them and slipping it into the lock. "Beachfront property."

Perhaps I've landed on my feet after all.

AA lets us into the house, and—*I'm glad*—flips on a light switch which brings up some bright, strip lighting. It's then that I realise we're standing in a kitchen; and not a *bad* kitchen at that:

Blue-white tiles that look fairly clean, with one of those artificial, plasticky wooden counters running along the surface.

A large fridge stands off over in the corner—one of those old-style, *chunky* models . . . the sort of fridge the contents of which would probably survive a nuclear holocaust.

The air inside smells a little of bacon—somewhat inexplicably—but I don't have time to really consider this detail in much depth as I notice the corridor leading off and away from the kitchen.

"This way," AA says, making off along the corridor.

I stand stunned for another few seconds, then snap to attention.

AA leads me past several closed doors, then past another one which is open and—when I look inside—I see contains a reasonably respectable bathroom.

I'll be making use of that later on, no doubt.

AA brings me to the last door at the end of the corridor and, without pausing, he turns the doorknob, then shoves his weight into a shoulder barge, as if he wants to pre-empt any idea the door has of becoming stuck.

He flips on another light and the whole room basks in a bright glow of electrical light.

I take in the pair of camp beds: one of them empty; the other occupied.

It takes me a swift moment to move my gaze from the empty camp bed—with its forest-green bedding and bobbly blankets—to the one alongside.

And, more precisely, to the occupant.

My eyes pass over the huddled-up form, stirring now.

I take in the blond hair, neatly arranged—even while she's sleeping—into a business-like bun on the top of her head. And then, as AA dumps my plastic bag containing all the possessions I brought along on this trip, I see her eyelids flutter open, those famous *blues* of hers blinking out at me.

Amy Douglas—Charlie Branwick's daughter . . . and—*apparently*—an ally.

But, before I have a chance to say her name, she says mine. "Anna?"

Chapter Twenty-Three

AMY QUICKLY bunches her knees up to her chest. She sits upright in bed, staring up at me. And then, as if AA has flicked another switch, she smiles wide and bright all of a sudden. "It's great to see you," she says, with a slight shake of her head, as if she's having trouble believing I'm really here. "You have no idea what these past few weeks have been like."

Although I don't have snark on my mind, I can't help but utter, "Did your house blow up too?"

Amy's smile falters for a second, then she meets my eye. Her blue eyes glitter in the harsh, too-bright light shed by the unshaded, naked bulb above our heads. She smiles wider than ever and, without warning, throws off her blankets and rushes to me.

Throws her tight, muscular body hard into my own.

Like a child who's just returned to her mother after months away.

She grabs tight to me, tugs me to her.

And I run my hand up her back, feel how hard she holds her muscles.

All tense.

When I eventually manage to prise myself away, and look back into her eyes, I see that they're sodden with tears.

"Anna," she says, with a shake of her head, "you have no idea what we're into."

I shift a glance off in AA's direction, noting that he's lurking voyeuristically, at the fringe of this encounter. "No, I really don't," I reply.

———

True to his word, AA cooks up some breakfast in the kitchen.

And although it doesn't look to be a patch on the sort of storms which Mark whips up, I'm glad that I don't have to cook on only a few hours' sleep.

He has shrugged off his jacket, hung it up on a jagged hook by the door, and rolled up his shirt sleeves to the elbow. He looks entirely business-like . . . apart, perhaps, from the apron which he's tied on to protect his—*rather nice*—suit trousers from rogue splashes of egg or bacon or coffee.

As I sit at the cobbled-together wooden table—something which Mark would, no doubt, have trouble *not* 'fixing'—I rest my elbows on the cheap plastic covering. This being Scotland, it has a plaid pattern to it: sort of Christmassy colours of green and red; gold and silver. I suppose it *is* getting on for that time of year.

If before I felt a little like a mother, now I feel more like a big sister, having come home from some big, scary adventure. I catch that sort of admiring gaze off Amy as she sits beside me.

This morning, Amy wears loose-fitting black cotton pyjamas.

She has tugged her hair free of its bun and, after tearing it apart with her fingers, it now hangs free about her shoulders, and down her back.

I can see a slight glow on the horizon—out to what I suppose to be the coast—as the sun begins to rise. Soon it'll be daytime and, hopefully, it'll go some way to mitigating the frightful chill which holds this seaside cottage in its grip.

As AA fries bacon, poaches eggs and boils away a kettle—cups of instant coffee at the ready—I turn to Amy, look her deep in the eye and say, "I'm only going to ask this once, all right?"

Amy fixes me with a stern glare . . . but one which, I can tell, deep down, is only put on for show. So that I'll *think* that she's being serious.

I hope that she does realise I *am* being serious.

Or else it might lead to greater problems later on.

"Can I trust you?" I say, and then, because I can tell that AA's listening in, I decide to amplify the enquiry. "Can I trust *all* of you?"

Before either AA or Amy can reply, I hear the *creak* of hinges off in the depths of the cottage. When I turn my attention in the direction of the sound, I see, shifting through the shadows, another form.

This time my brain reaches its conclusion faster.

I realise that—dressed in a fluffy white dressing gown; red hair fixed back in a ponytail—it's Tabby.

She gives me a thin-lipped smile before settling down on the other side of the table from me and Amy. "Morning," she just about gets out as she sinks down on the chair. She shifts a glance off in AA's direction. "You know the walls in this place really are paper-thin"—she reaches out and peels back a loose piece of wallpaper—"should probably have thought about reinforcing the walls while you were redecorating."

"Yeah?" AA says tilting his head back in her direction, but not turning around from his breakfast efforts. "Funny thing, you know, Amy didn't mention that over the phone."

I sense just a touch of friction in the air, between Tabby and AA; and I have to admit that I'm not unhappy to feel it . . . it stops things from seeming just a little too chummy.

And—if there's one thing I hate—it's people getting too chummy behind my back.

Before I get the chance to ask my 'trust question' again, AA begins serving up the poached eggs and bacon. I see that each of us has buttered wholemeal toast to go with our breakfast.

It seems that AA's really going to be taking care of us.

Chapter Twenty-Four

ONCE BREAKFAST IS DONE WITH, and I'm feeling nice and full—if not a little exhausted—AA chases me out of the kitchen and back to the bedroom I seem set to share with Amy.

He stands about in the doorway for a moment or two, before I think to say to him, "It's okay—I think I can find the bathroom for myself."

He gives me a nod and then heads back to the kitchen, where the washing-up awaits.

I have a quick shower, of which my main complaint is that there's not a whole lot of pressure, but the water's hot so maybe I should just count my blessings. There's a lemon-scented shower gel, too, which I make good use of. And which has the effect of giving my body another kick, after that strong coffee AA served me at breakfast.

Once I'm all towelled off, I slip on a fresh, clean white t-shirt over a pair of waterproof trousers—the types which're favoured by people enjoying extreme sports . . . or just *walkers.* The trousers are a sort of sludge-green colour, but they're nice and comfortable so I think I'll manage.

It's not like, out here, all this way Up North, there's going to be anybody I know to criticise what I've happened to put on this particular morning.

Only AA who—it's true—*can* be quite scathing with his criticisms.

I put on my denim jacket over the top of my outfit and, even without a mirror to check on my appearance, I know that it's going to be a decently sized fashion faux pas.

. . . *Whatever.*

Back in the kitchen, I find myself confronting Amy—who's already dressed herself, apparently having skipped the shower. She wears a pair of worn-in jeans with a peach-coloured blouse over the top; one button undone to show off her slender, feather-white throat. Her blond hair hangs down to one side; fine and well-combed. It reminds me a little of tassels . . . but I don't say that out loud—I suppose that sort of comment could quite easily be interpreted as an insult.

Although Amy's certainly dressed down, I can't help but notice that she's done so in a quite self-conscious way—wanting to ensure that she looks *presentable*, at the very least.

I don't know quite who Amy's trying to impress with her appearance.

The seagulls?

I glance to the kitchen sink, see that the plates from breakfast have already been neatly stacked up. I guess that I should make a point of never underestimating AA's washing-and-drying skills . . . or perhaps he had a helping hand from Tabby.

Feeling a touch tentative about this whole situation, I give

Amy a pleasant smile and then lower myself down into one of the seats at the kitchen table.

"Nice shower?" she says.

"Uh-huh," I reply, meeting her eye for a second and then drifting away from her gaze—casting my attention over that ginormous, pre-historic fridge. "How long have you been here?"

"Oh," Amy says, her eyes lolling upwards in their sockets. "About a week."

"What about AA and Tabby?" I say.

"AA drove me up here in the first place—Tabby arrived yesterday afternoon."

"What're you doing all the way up here?"

Amy shrugs her shoulders, meets my eye a second and then looks away.

"Amy?" I say.

"Mm?" she says, smiling once more when she looks back at me.

"You know that thing I said, about *trust*?"

"Yeah."

"Well, this is one of those times when you can prove it to me."

Amy looks me back in the eye, and then away again. She breathes in deeply and then sighs out. "This is my dad's place," she says.

My gut tightens a few notches.

"It's okay," she says, with a smile. "I told him that I was coming up here. He knows where I am—and it'll be the last place that he thinks to look for any of you."

"And why're you *up here*?" I say.

She gives another shrug. "I thought that it'd be a good place for us to hide out for a while, so that we'd have some time to plot our next move."

" '*Our*' next move?" I say, deeply aware that I haven't yet signed up for anything.

At least I *hope* I haven't.

"Yeah," Amy says, and then frowns. "Didn't AA tell you about what's going on, about the plan?"

"I think you should just assume that I know nothing at all. The only thing I know is that somebody burned down my house —*maybe they tried to bomb it*—and that it'd be nice to find out who precisely did it . . . or, if not, to be left alone to live out the rest of my life without needing to glance back over my shoulder the whole time." I arch my shoulders, bring my hands up onto the table then interlock my fingers. "To not feel that out there—*some-where*—there's a bullet with my name on it."

Amy smirks. "Well, if you want to talk about the truth of the thing, there's a bullet out there for *all* of us."

"Maybe," I say, "but that doesn't mean that I can't at least *try* to seek assurances." I turn my attention back onto Amy—*full glare*. "So, tell me, what's the plan?"

Amy gives me a naughty little smile, one of those which, I'm sure, she has carried around with her ever since she was a young girl . . . one of those smiles which just screams that she's been caught with her hand in the cookie jar.

"To bring down Brian Mathewson, of course."

Chapter Twenty-Five

WHILE ME AND AMY sit in the kitchen, she goes through the entire plan—what we're going to do next. How—*exactly*—we're going to go about bringing down Brian Mathewson's empire for good. And thus ensure our—and not to mention the nation's—safety forever more.

Or so goes the theory.

She details out how we're going to take out a series of strategic targets—people who're close to Brian; and who would be capable of stopping us—before taking out Brian himself.

The key, as Amy explains, is that Brian has built in all sorts of insurance policies for his company, Mathewson Media; young upstarts who are very much in Brian's mould and who're more than ready to take up the mantle if and when required.

Actually more like *eager* and *chomping at the bit.*

Then—and only then—when all of Brian's support systems are gone, will we be able to turn our attention to Brian himself.

When Amy reaches the end of her explanation, leaving me

feeling not a little punch-drunk by the whole experience, she draws in a gasp that makes me think that she might've broken a nail.

In the end, though, she reaches out across the table, completely subconsciously, and grabs for my hand. "Lizzie," Amy says, eyebrows raised. "Is she okay?"

I feel myself warming inside, just to think of my fuzzy—*furry* —companion. "Yes," I say, "she's fine."

"Where is she?" Amy says. "Did you bring her with you?"

I shake my head; inform Amy that she's staying with friends.

And Amy seems to buy that story just fine.

She doesn't press me for an exact location—*names and places*— nothing like that.

Though I imagine that if she asked AA where Lizzie is then AA would only be too happy to tell her. Just because he can.

After about half an hour or so of me and Amy lurking in the kitchen, AA thinks to show his face, having had a shower himself. Dressed down now, wearing a thick, navy-blue knitted jumper over the top of some nicely creased, deep-purple corduroy trousers.

Tabby, too, emerges.

She has on a yellow turtleneck sweater over the top of a flowing skirt with lavender patterns stencilled onto it. She wears a pair of moleskin boots, which come up to just below her kneecaps.

The way that she stands, her red hair casually flowing and resting on her shoulder blades, she looks as if she simply woke up that way.

I suppose I should be grateful that I know the truth for myself, having seen her earlier that morning in her dressing gown.

With all of us standing about in the same place, AA proposes that we go outside for a walk along the beachfront.

For a Scottish winter's day, I can see, out the window, that there's searing blue skies and the waves are sparkling in the weak sunlight.

Even looking at that sight, though, I know that it'll be bitterly cold the second that I place one foot over the threshold.

And so it proves to be.

I pace alongside Amy while Tabby and AA stalk along, up ahead, the two of them with their heads bowed, expressions solemn, as if the weight of the world balances on their shoulders.

Perhaps they shouldn't be so melodramatic since—in all likelihood—it's only the weight of the *country* which hangs on them.

But I keep my mind off it.

As we walk the concrete seawall, beside the foaming sea, waves crash into shore, tearing up the pebble beach. And I can't help but realise just how alone we are out here.

No matter how hard I look, I can't make out another house on the hillside.

Only the wild, long-growing grasses.

All of them blowing around in the breeze.

Already, I can feel the ocean air restoring me, as if it breathes new life directly into my lungs. Every step that I take seems lighter than the last one . . . and I can't help wondering if I haven't—*somehow*—entered some sort of fantasy movie; that, at any second, without warning, I might be about to take flight.

Just to be sure, I reach out and grasp tight to the white railing —its paintjob flaking away—which creates a barrier between us and the pebble beach about ten, fifteen metres below.

The air seems to grow frostier with each step, too, and pretty soon I find myself having no choice *except* to embrace the cold.

As I walk along, I feel my heart beating slow and steady, and I fix my attention on Amy, who has, from somewhere, summoned a duffel coat with toggles. She trudges along the seawall with her hands firmly inserted in the pockets—a little rosiness coming out in her cheeks.

"So," I say, determined to strike up some sort of conversation, "your dad didn't mind much about you snuffing that woman"—I pretend to struggle to recall her name—"*Grendelin*, back on the island?"

Hands still firmly placed in her pockets, Amy hunches her shoulders. "Nah," she says, then slips me a sidelong glance. "I mean, he never found out."

I give a slight pout. "And you never thought to explain?"

Amy gives a quick shake of her head, and we pace onwards.

Along the seawall.

As we go along, I attempt to track snatches of Tabby and AA's conversation, but can only catch the odd word, here and there. I can tell, just from their tone of voice, that they're speaking extremely determinedly about—what I intuit to be —the Plan.

"Anna," Amy says, almost out of nowhere.

"Yeah?" I say, turning into her.

Amy comes to a stop. She stares out to sea, out into the murky, grey depths; the surface just about illuminated by the weak winter sunshine, and then she turns her back to it—looks me in the eye.

And I find myself getting lost in her blue eyes for several seconds.

What she does to the boys, I *really* don't want to know.

I glance along the seawall, see that AA and Tabby are continuing on their way, apparently unaware that me and Amy have stopped at all.

"You said we had to be truthful," Amy says. "So here goes."

I feel my gut clench, just *knowing* that I'm going to live to regret that particular taking-of-the-moral-high-ground.

Amy goes on, "It's about Grendelin, about what I told my father."

Already, I have an inkling of what this is going to be.

And to say I don't much like it is an understatement.

"I told my dad that *you* killed her—that was the reason why he made you a target; why he decided to make you his Enemy Number One." She holds my gaze for another few seconds, and then looks off out to sea once more.

"I'm sorry that I said it, but there didn't seem to be another choice. You see, I need my dad to believe that I'm still on his side. That I *only* want to fight with him. He already needed an explanation for me staying behind on the island, for not taking the flight out with him."

She sniffs a laugh, but soon draws it right back in as if she herself realises that it was somewhat premature. "That was the only way for us to keep an eye on Brian Mathewson, with *me* on the inside." She shakes her head. "I never expected it to come to this—AA paid off the assassin for as long as he could manage . . . and then, when that was gone, I took from my dad's own money to try and keep you safe."

I decide this is my opportunity to break in. "That money which AA's desperate to pay back—that's from your father, isn't it?"

Amy nods in reply. "Yes," she says. "He hasn't *quite* cottoned on yet, but he's certainly been sniffing around. He's been investigating where that money ended up . . . not to mention attempting to work out what became of his hired assassin—why he didn't go through with the hit."

For a second I forget myself—forget the gravity of the situation.

I smirk. "Paying off an assassin with the same money used to hire him—*nice*." The two of us reflect on this in silence for a matter of moments, then I say, "Did your dad set the bomb?"

"I don't know, Anna," Amy replies, still staring out to sea. "I don't know that for sure."

Amy grows so still that I'm afraid she might have frozen to death in the frosty air. On a whim, I reach out and touch her on the shoulder. "Whenever you need the money—just let me know. I'll wire it to you straight away. Nothing can be more important than us covering our tracks now."

Amy gives me a smile. The skin about her eyes crinkles. Then she reaches out and clasps hold of my hand, gives it a squeeze. "Thanks," she says. "Thanks for being so understanding."

"Don't mention it," I say. "It's almost Christmas, after all."

Chapter Twenty-Six

W E WALK ALL THE WAY along the seawall, over to an outcropping of black rocks: the natural landmark for the end of the pebble beach.

Already, on the horizon, I can make out black clouds forming.

I suppose that Scotland will always be *Scotland.*

AA meets my eye, and gives me a smile which doesn't convince. "Head back?" he says.

I think about the cottage awaiting us, and I can't help but hope that—*just perhaps*—there'll be some hot chocolate stowed away in a cupboard somewhere.

On the way back along the seawall, me and Amy say nothing at all to one another.

We only trudge on in silence.

When we're about half of the way back to the cottage, I'm surprised to feel Amy's gentle fingertips brush up against the sleeve of my denim jacket. And then, without so much as a muttered word, she loops her arm through mine, so that we must look—to Tabby and AA tailing our heels—like a pair of elderly women keeping one another company.

Back in the cottage, I'm pleased when AA digs out—*from somewhere*—an electric heater. He sets it up before the kitchen table so that us girls: me, Amy and Tabby; can all get ourselves warmed up after having been out in the adverse weather.

Unfortunately there's no hot chocolate to be had. As Amy explains, her father has a heart condition so he's on doctor's orders to stay away from sweets. There are, however, lots of teabags, and AA wastes no time in putting on the kettle and getting a brew going.

If there's one thing which can solve most miseries in life, it's tea.

As the warmth from the electric heater ekes out from its metal frame, I feel myself begin to sweat. I undo my denim jacket a touch—to allow some of the draught to brush up against my skin; to give me some sort of cooling.

I find myself tickled just to reflect on the sight of us—all *four of us*—hanging about the kitchen of Amy's father's cottage in Scotland.

Just how did we manage to get here?

How did we manage to get caught up in this?

How did we get ourselves involved with Brian Mathewson?

But there's no doubt that we did . . .

Me, with my mousy-brown hair. Amy the blonde. Tabby the redhead. And, finally, AA with his slicked back, apparently, weatherproof black hair which glistens a little in the kitchen light, probably owing to the lashings of gel that he's no doubt smothered it with.

Maybe we should audition for TV when this is all over.

Or not . . . I can imagine that all four of us will be well and truly done with media for a while once we've got this thing over and done with.

When we've finally taken care of Brian Mathewson.

Once we've got the tea down our throats—and I'm mighty glad, at least for me, that I've done that much—the group's attention shifts back, once more, to the Plan.

Before we get into the intricacies of it, though, AA glances across the table at me, a frown clinging to his lips. "Anna, did you bring the memory stick?"

"Hmm?" I say, half hypnotised by the warm tea which is currently swilling about my guts, warming me from within. "Oh, the Death Log?"

"The 'Death' what?" Tabby puts in.

I flap my hand at the air as if it wasn't important . . . and, to me, it really wasn't. "It's just the name that I give the memory stick; gives it a little more character."

"A bit morbid, don't you think?" AA says, furrowing his eyebrows.

I resist the urge to pull up AA—*a professional assassin*—for moralising.

I shrug. "Dunno, makes it more distinct from most memory sticks, I suppose."

"Right," AA says, and then drains the remainder of his cup of tea, "but you've got it with you now?"

I glance about the table, feeling all three of them with their eyes on me.

That impromptu lecture I gave them about the virtue of telling the truth returns to me.

But, this time, I tell myself that I have a good reason.

A good reason for lying.

"Yeah, in my bag," I say, and then wait for AA to ask to see it. But he doesn't follow up.

He only gives me a stern nod, and then moves the conversation onto the next matter.

As I sit there, at the table, on the rickety wooden chair, I feel their words washing over me. There's a lot of talk of guns and targets and getaways; all of these things that I—*sincerely*—believed I had managed to escape.

Those things that I thought Brian had excused me from for the rest of my life.

At the same time, though, I know that all my involvement in this really isn't Amy's fault. That she *did* have to tell her father something. And telling him that I was the one to kill Grendelin sounds only reasonable. It's really just the nature of the business.

No matter where I run to, no matter how hard I try to bury my head in the sand, it'll always find a way to haul me back in.

Unlike the assassination jobs which Brian dealt us, there're no folders on the targets. Tabby and AA have already memorised not only their own missions, and the intricacies of said missions, but they also know about mine and Amy's in elaborate detail.

They ask me and Amy to memorise all that they tell us.

And—I have to admit—I tune out of the conversation somewhat as AA continues to drawl on and on. At one point, he has to call my name—who knows how many times?—before I finally turn to meet his eye. When he finally does look at me, I feel almost as if I've gone back to school and the teacher's calling on me to give some answer.

"Anna?" AA says. "Are you okay with that?"

"Okay with what?" I say, stifling a yawn with the back of my hand, and, over AA's shoulder, seeing that the black clouds have all settled in over the beach.

In a matter of minutes, we'll be set for *some* storm.

"With taking care of Brian Mathewson?"

It hits me almost like a punch to the solar plexus.

I feel winded for several moments.

And then I look back to AA. "Taking care of Brian?"

AA gives me a stern nod in reply. "Can you handle it?"

I feel Amy, Tabby and AA's eyes all on me.

Waiting for my response.

Waiting to see if I'll agree to do it.

If I'm as cold blooded as they've, no doubt, heard on the grapevine.

Chapter Twenty-Seven

A S THE STORM MOVES IN over the cottage, I lie on
the camp bed, in the room I share with Amy. Already, I
can hear Amy's heavy breathing—I know that she's already off in
the land of dreams; already away from everything that's going
on here.

I wish that I could find sleep so easily.

It's so much to take in.

I can hear the rain drumming away against the roof tiles, can
hear it *tinkling* into the stainless-steel drainpipes. The falling rain
seems almost to draw out the damp from the rest of the cottage
—to make it thick and almost impenetrable to breathe.

But there seems very little option.

My mouth tastes salty from the noodles which AA—*again*—
rustled up for dinner . . . I wonder if this cooking compulsion of
his is something which has always been present or if it's the kind
of condition which only manifests itself in times of crisis.

After we had our meeting, Amy instructed all of us to remove the batteries from our mobile phones. To do the same with any other tech we'd brought along with us. Only Tabby—I saw—brought along a laptop, and I observed as she pulled out the battery pack, wrapped it up carefully in a kitchen towel before depositing it in the fridge.

With a smile, she told me that it would help the battery to keep its life.

Keep it from becoming damaged.

I guess that I learn something new every day . . .

Amy went on to say that this was a measure to ensure that none of us would be tracked. That our digital footprint would've led us up here, to this cottage in the middle of nowhere. And that's where we'll remain to the best of any *snooper's* knowledge. Only we won't be here for much longer.

Sometimes I feel almost stranded in this modern, digital world.

Unable to quite fathom all its tricks and intricacies.

I fired off a message to Mark, managing—*somehow*—to get signal by standing upright on the foot of my bed, waving my phone in the air so that it almost touched the ceiling. Then I did as Amy instructed, removing the battery pack from the phone. Not bothering with Tabby's trick of leaving it in the fridge, instead deciding that the battery will be just fine at the bottom of my plastic bag.

I stretch out my legs, feeling the tough, over-washed bedsheet of the camp bed rubbing against my bare ankles. There's something cosy about sleeping in the same room as Amy, as if I've just gone away to camp for the weekend with my Brownies group.

Except I never *joined* Brownies.

Once all the mobile-phone business was done with, AA took me around back just as the rain began to fall. There was a wood shed. When I noted that there was no open fire within the cottage, AA explained how Amy's father would have fires down on the beach.

That this was the reason for the wood being there.

Even as we approached the wood shed, I noticed how the padlock looked brand new; that there was none of the rust which I might've expected.

And perhaps I should've known.

Because where there's a fresh, newly bought—*extremely secure* —lock on a wood shed there's surely something really quite *valuable* within.

Or else something really quite *dangerous.*

I can still picture in my mind as AA slipped the key into the slot on the padlock. There was that satisfying *click* within the mechanism. And there I was—*naïve old me!*—still believing that there might just be wood in the shed.

But, no.

When AA brought the door open, showed me the interior, sure enough, I took in the arsenal which he kept there; rifles, handguns, a couple of smoke grenades. All the equipment someone might need to arm a small uprising.

And, well, I suppose that this *is*—in its way—an uprising.

But it's certainly *not* small.

Although AA said nothing as he lingered in the doorway, his eyes alive for any motion outside of the shed, even though the countryside was *obviously* deserted, I pried about inside and picked out a pair of forty-five calibre handguns which took my fancy.

And it was only when I met AA's eye, realised how intently he was staring at me, that I twigged that this woodshed here—well, no way around it—belonged to none other than Amy's father. That this was his own little home from home.

Just in case any burglars came to call.

He could slip in and grab himself something to defend his homestead with.

Guns picked out, and with my ammo selected, AA nodded to me and allowed me out of the wood shed: my new friends alongside me.

Without another word, he locked the wood shed, before glancing about suspiciously again.

Sometimes I wonder if AA just likes to see me squirm.

If he just likes to put me on edge.

Maybe he believes—*deep down*—that it's the best way I operate.

As for me, I'm not so sure.

I *never* feel like I quite perform my best.

But, with the target now being Brian Mathewson, I know that nothing short of my best will do.

I lie back on the camp bed, feeling the spring-loaded mattress slinking away beneath me, somehow never quite settling into a normally formed shape.

When I turn on my side, I feel a little better.

Like I can finally shut my eyes.

And *try* to drift off.

But I don't get very far.

Because—*outside*—clear as day, I hear a twig snapping beneath a boot.

My eyes rip wide open.

And I scream out into the darkness.

Chapter Twenty-Eight

I THROW MYSELF onto the ground just in time.

Bullets pound into the walls of the cottage.

A burst of gunfire.

I just about have the presence of mind to reach out and grab hold of Amy—sitting up straight in her bed—brought around from her dreaming.

When I have her down on the floor beside me, I jerk her head into my chest, as if she was one of my children, afraid of a thunderstorm. The two of us lie there, huddled up, waiting for the cacophony to cease.

But the bullets keep coming.

Until they're curtailed by a shout outside.

I know that we need to move quickly, that there's no time for me and Amy to get complacent. That we need to keep our wits about us. I jabber at Amy, demand that she grabs hold of her gun—*wherever the hell it is*. She scrabbles about for seemingly minutes and I know that, in this situation, in this scenario, that variables can change so quickly that Amy's delay might mean our death.

As for me, I already have my gun.

I lie there, eyes fixed on the bedroom door, waiting for some gun-toting nutter to come through. Ready to line up the headshot.

But nobody comes.

My heart flutters up to my throat.

My blood runs hot—and then impossibly cold.

My skin, all of a sudden, seems slick with sweat.

My palms, too, are sweating.

I take my hands off my gun for a quick moment, wipe the sweat from my palms onto the tatty old shirt I wear to bed. Then I fix my attention back on the doorway, telling myself that they could come at any time. And that I can't be *anything* but ready.

Outside, I tune back into the muffled voices.

I guess their position:

Rounding the cottage.

Heading for the outside door which leads into the kitchen.

I wonder what sort of a state they've left AA's car in. Did they take some sort of vengeance on it before they opened fire?

Right now, it really doesn't matter.

All that matters is that we're ready.

That we're *prepared.*

I glance to the bedroom door again, realise that I can hear some sound out in the hallway. I move quickly, crawling on my front. When I reach the door, I get up on my knees, reach for the doorknob. Turn it as quietly as I can manage, waiting for—*any second*—when the gunfire will start up again . . . when the bullets will tear through me.

When that bullet with my name on it will—*finally*—find me.

I get the door open then peer out into the hallway.

It's dark, of course. We turned off all the lights before we ventured to bed.

We never expected to have company tonight, but now that we do, it seems to have worked out well not to leave any lights on. Good thing none of us is afraid of the dark.

I remain on my front, gun out ahead of me.

Over my shoulder, I can hear Amy fumbling through dresser drawers and I want to tell her to stop it. But, at the same time, I know that it would only make more of a noise for me to chide her than to just leave her to it.

Hey, if she bites the bullet, she bites the bullet.

Survival of the fittest.

. . . Even then—even in that fraught moment—I realise just how cold that sounds.

Out in the hallway now, feeling the freezing linoleum floor press up against my cheek, I spot AA. Like me, he has his gun drawn. But he is crouched, in the doorway of his bedroom, staring back into the kitchen, waiting for the door to spring open.

Looking a little further along the hallway, I see that Tabby is there, too.

Her own gun drawn.

I allow myself a slight smile.

I convince myself that we'll catch them off guard.

That we'll have the upper hand here.

Only time will tell for sure, of course.

I wait there, breathing deep, trying to get my heart rate under control.

That's the trick.

I just need to think *calm* thoughts.

Then my body will follow.

I hear the scraping of a key at the kitchen's exterior door.

And it's then that I hear Amy's voice over my shoulder.

Even as I glance back at her with the scowl on my lips, I find myself wondering if I should fire a bullet through her windpipe to keep her quiet.

"Anna!" she says, in a husky whisper. "Anna! Put your gun down!"

I have *zero* intention of doing that.

"Listen," she says, the key still scraping about in the lock . . . I wonder what's giving them so much trouble—perhaps AA changed the locks. "Just give yourselves up—you have no idea . . . no idea . . ."

But, right then, the key turns in the kitchen door.

And the door itself busts open.

Gunfire fills the air.

Chapter Twenty-Nine

I FEEL my whole body go rigid.

There's too many of them—*far too many.*

And they all wear body armour.

Helmets with visors drawn down.

All of them carry automatic rifles.

I notice, almost right away, that they're not shooting *at* us, that they're firing warning shots up into the ceiling. Paintwork —*plaster*—comes floating down like snowflakes. I have no option but to lay my gun down . . . not unless I want to sign my own execution order.

And apparently me, Tabby and AA all have exactly the same thought, at the same time.

Because we all lay our guns down before us—on the ground.

I follow the barked instructions.

To lie on my front, hands behind my back.

Ready to be cuffed.

As I lie there, on the floor, I look to Amy.

I look for any trace of a knowing smile—of having become ensnared in her trap for the umpteenth time. And yet I can see nothing. Nothing there at all. Either she's a terrific actress or she's just as surprised by this raid as the rest of us.

But no way am I jumping to conclusions just yet.

That's a *recipe* for trouble.

The men in armoured vests—*police?*—hold their guns up in their arms, in the Ready position, just looking for a target to fire on. Just daring one of us to step out of line.

I think back to earlier that evening, when Amy told us all to turn off our phones, to remove the batteries so that we wouldn't be tracked when we headed back down south.

I guess that we were just a little slow pulling *that* trick.

As I hear a succession of, "Clear!" pass all the way through the cottage, and feel the rub of cold steel against my wrists—that somewhat fatal *snap* of the lock being engaged—a tremor passes through my gut.

Because I know this is the end.

This is *how* it ends.

And, for once, there's absolutely nothing I can do about it.

As one of the armoured men tugs me up to my feet, I think about all those times when I *might* have died . . . and about how none of those moments compare to now.

We're out here—*in the middle of nowhere*—and at the whim of men with guns.

It couldn't get any worse.

Could it?

Right then, as I stagger forwards, my hands cuffed behind my back, the force of the armoured man holding onto the back of my shirt, I notice another figure walking in through the door. A somewhat *familiar* figure.

It takes me a moment to process his features.

For my brain to fully take him in:

Bald head.

Puffed-out chest.

About in his mid-fifties.

Like all the others, he wears an armoured vest, but he has on no helmet; and, instead of a rifle, he has a sidearm, holstered, down at his thigh.

When his eyes cross mine, his face remains dour, and he says, "If you wanted to borrow the cottage, you had only to ask."

Amy's father.

Charlie Branwick.

Chapter Thirty

B Y ALL RIGHTS, I should want to scratch Amy's eyes out. Because somehow—*somehow*—she has fooled us once again.

And there we were, talking about trust.

As if it might've meant something.

But I just can't summon the energy.

Perhaps something deep within me—dare I say a long-dormant *conscience?*—tells me that that won't solve anything. That killing Amy, despite being a practical impossibility right now, really won't help us out of this situation.

The armoured man shoves me out into the night, and I feel my bare feet make contact with the freezing-cold gravel driveway. There must be a layer of frost on the ground tonight. At first my whole body flashes with the pain, as I feel the grit dig into the soft soles of my feet.

But then I grow used to it.

I almost begin to think that I *deserve* it.

I have been an awfully naughty girl, after all.

Outside, I eye the cars.

All of them unmarked.

And all of them the same estate model—each of them with a sleek, black finish. Their bodywork shines in the moonlight.

There must be half a dozen cars.

One thing is for certain, Charlie Branwick—Amy's father—has come along prepared.

Which is more than can be said of us . . . of me, AA and Tabby.

The man in the armoured vest throws me hard against the wall of the cottage, tells me to stay put. And his rifle adds an unsubtle, 'You'd better.'

My eyes trace Tabby and AA as they approach; as they're thrown beside me.

Both look as shocked by what's happened as I feel.

Neither of them expected discovery.

For some reason, I cast my eyes over AA's choice of night-wear: a pair of golden silk pyjamas.

Despite myself—*despite the situation*—I can't suppress a slight chuckle within my ribs.

With a shake of my head, I tell myself that at least AA knows how to go out in style.

That if he's going down in flames then—*dammit*—he's going down wrapped in gold.

All of our eyes turn back to the kitchen door, though; and I observe Amy emerging.

It surprises me to see that she's wearing handcuffs, too.

Although, unlike me, AA and Tabby; she wears them around front, at her belly.

Perhaps it's only for show.

So that Amy won't need to illustrate—once and for all—that she's betrayed us until her father has put a bullet into each of our heads.

Then he'll let her out of her handcuffs and they'll cackle like villains over our lined-up corpses.

Charlie Branwick is the one who escorts his own daughter. He drags her along by her handcuffs before finally leaving us beside the rest of us, up against the wall.

I expect something from Amy, that she might at least make *some* effort to apologise, that she might *try* to make out that she's just as surprised about all of this as the rest of us.

But she simply stands straight-backed, up against the wall of the cottage, facing forwards.

I watch on as Charlie Branwick issues orders to his men.

Most of them disappear into the cottage; he leaves only a couple outside, to stand at his shoulders, no doubt so that they look threatening.

Charlie Branwick quickly deals that lingering pair of guards their orders, though. And although I can't hear his Glaswegian accent, I can tell from the context, from all the waggling of his finger in the direction of the sea, that they're to escort us down to the seawall.

At least I'll die with the sound of the sea ringing in my ears.

The guards nudge AA and Tabby away from the wall first. One of the guards tails them, as they head down to the sea. And then the other guard—the only one remaining outside the cottage—grabs hold of my handcuffs, leading me after AA and Tabby.

I manage one *final* look to Amy.

She won't even look me in the eye.

Her cheeks seem puffed out . . . as if she's awaiting her chance to burst out into maniacal laughter with her father.

Well, I suppose she's *earned* it.

She really has run rings around all three of us mental-wise.

Not that I've ever considered myself any sort of genius . . .

The men lead us along the seawall, and I notice—my mind on some sort of a skittish track now—that AA's wearing a pair of suede slippers.

At least he won't die with his dogs barking.

The pair of men line up the three of us against the railing.

With the sea to our backs.

They have the honour to look us in the face as they snuff our lives out.

But they don't do anything.

Not *yet*.

I don't know quite what grips a hold of me, but I find myself speaking out. "Go on," I say. "Why don't you get it over with?" I pause—swallow hard. "*Get paid!*"

I have to admit that it's not exactly my *best* line.

And the irony of the whole situation doesn't exactly work to my benefit, either.

But, I suppose, in the real world, we don't get to choose our exit speeches.

Neither of the guards says a word.

They both keep their guns held up.

Pointed at us.

I wonder which one of the three of us isn't in their sight.

A one in three shot that it's *not* me.

I might be able to get away a couple of steps before the bullet rips through my skull.

If I'm lucky.

148

I look back to the cottage on the hillside, about fifty, sixty paces away from where the guards have us all lined up for the execution.

And it's then that everything seems to move in slow motion.

As I watch it unfold, I'm baffled.

One second, I see Amy speaking with her father; the next, the whole world shakes.

The ground tumbles out from underneath my feet.

And I'm flat on the floor.

I think that's it . . . that this is what getting shot in the head feels like.

Only one thing is out of whack:

I'm still alive.

Chapter Thirty-One

I FEEL the heat up against my face.

Almost too much to bear.

I can feel a great light splashing against my closed eyelids.

Redness fills my vision—takes away my senses.

In my imagination, I see my house burning down before my eyes. I feel the tickle of ash tumbling past my face; its hot cinders making contact with my skin. When I draw a breath, all I can breathe is ash. It's as if it fills my lungs.

I wonder if this is hell—if I've finally made it here.

But then I try to beat that thought from my mind.

Because I *am* still alive.

I reach about me, feel the solid ground. The seawall. The steady concrete.

Then I glance to the slumped-over forms:

To Tabby.

To AA.

Both of them sprawled on the ground beside me.

When I look out ahead, past the tips of my toes, I see the guards who're meant to be watching us. They, too, lie on their fronts.

For some reason, my eyes only drift over to the blazing inferno at the very last.

Up there, on the hill.

So enormous—so much in *centre stage*—that it's impossible to miss.

Flame seems to spurt from all over the cottage.

Out of the windows.

Out of the doors.

Out through the roof.

And the area around back, the gravel drive, too, is alive with flame.

That's when something switches in my brain.

I find myself thinking, *Amy*!

And perhaps it's because my brain hasn't quite snagged onto the fact that Amy is the enemy, that she betrayed us all . . . and not for the first time . . . but I thrust myself forwards, taking long strides, determined to reach the cottage so that I might . . . *what?*

Save her?

Yes! That's what I tell myself.

That I need to *save* her.

I pump my legs, feeling the solid concrete beneath my bare feet, and the flame growing hotter against my face as I go. When I get closer to the burning cottage, I see some forms within, nothing much more than blackened mannequins—*silhouettes*; burning to death.

A veritable barbecue.

I turn my attention to the last place I saw Amy, and I catch sight of her, lying on the ground, thrown a good ten paces clear of the cottage. I keep myself low, trying to shield myself from the impossibly hot blaze. When I reach her side, I crouch down.

Right as I'm about to grab hold of her hand, to give it a squeeze, I stop myself.

Something catches my attention.

Something *in* Amy's hand.

I tilt my head, getting a better look at it.

A device—something which looks a little like a car key fob . . . one of those remote-control deals, like the one which AA has for his canary-yellow sports car.

I lean in closer to inspect it, and I see that there's a distinct button on the top, and that Amy's finger is locked tight down upon it.

Squeezing it into the device.

It's then that Amy's eyelids flutter. She widens her eyes several times, and then her focus appears to find me. Her lips part a fraction and she says, "Anna . . . is that you?"

"Yes," I say, and then I do reach out for Amy's hand.

And when she grips onto my hand she squeezes hard.

I tug her up to her feet, prevent her from keeling right over onto her side.

When I look around, for Amy's father—*for Charlie Branwick*—I see his body lying several paces away. It takes me a minute or so to realise that he's missing a good portion of his scalp; that said good portion of scalp lies a distance away.

I take a firm hold of Amy, not allowing her to look back.

Nobody should see their parents like this.

As I lead her back towards the seawall, a prospect shakes me. That although the explosion—*whatever the hell just happened here*—has done for the other body-armoured men, those guards, the ones which were keeping tabs on me, AA and Tabby, are still very much in action.

Amy mumbles under her breath. I can't make out a word she says. All I can think to do is reach up and stroke her blond hair, and it's there that I feel a slight dampness. When I snatch a glance at the side of her head, I see blood seeping out through her hair.

I put that out of my mind for the moment.

We can lick our wounds in a moment's time.

As we draw closer to Tabby and AA—and the guards, of course—I see that they're just coming around. And that the guards are still out cold.

Taking care, I set Amy down on a grassy bank, and then quickly see to the guards. As I make short work of disarming them, as they make various grumbles and grunts, I speculate that —if I'd been thinking one-hundred-per-cent clearly—I might've thought to disarm the guards as my first port of call.

Still, action is as action demands.

There was no time for me to think things through, and seeing to Amy seemed more urgent than keeping Tabby and AA from a sticky fate.

Although I tell myself there'll be time to do so later, I can't help but think on my motivation. Think about why I went off to go and save a would-be traitor rather than protect my *True Friends*.

But Amy didn't turn out to be a traitor at all . . .

I stand back, waiting for the various people before me to come around.

I keep an eye on the cottage burning away behind me, very much aware that—at any second—some well-meaning man in an armoured vest might emerge from the wreckage taking pot shots at us.

Finally, I watch as AA and Tabby come around from their daze. Just like Amy did, they blink away their shock. They look up onto the hillside, become hypnotised by the sight of the burning cottage, and then turn back to me; as if *I'm* going to offer them some sort of explanation beyond spontaneous combustion.

"What . . . happened?" AA says, rubbing his head and squinting beyond me, once more, to the burning building.

I feel the warmth of the blaze causing me to sweat—a somewhat surreal sensation on a cold winter's night such as this one. I open my mouth to say something, and it's only then that I realise I have nothing to say.

That I *have no idea* . . . other than speculation.

Thankfully, Amy has regained enough of her consciousness to fill us in. "A bomb," she says, as if it was *obvious* . . . as if that one word just explains everything.

I look to AA and Tabby, to see if Amy's explanation gives them anything at all to work with.

But they look just as clueless as I feel.

Amy has some *serious* explaining to do.

Chapter Thirty-Two

W E SIT THERE, basking in the glow of the burning cottage, with the ash falling all around. I hear some of the cinders *sizzle* as they meet with the surface of the sea. I keep a watchful eye fixed on the pair of armoured men—neither of them armed now, of course, but I'm not about to kid myself that they're not dangerous.

Amy looks me in the eye, and then she says, "We agreed that all of us would tell the truth from now on, so that's what I'm going to do." She draws a deep breath, as if she's about to start up a hundred-metre sprint . . . as if she's got every intention of shooting for gold. Her eyes go dead, almost opaque. And I can tell that there must be just about a million things zipping through her mind right now. "I brought them up here," she says, "with the mobile phones—I knew that they'd be coming."

She gives a shake of her head. "I'm sorry that I couldn't say anything at the time . . . it just would've made things more complicated; it would've caused more . . . more *trust* issues.

"I had my dad, and his group, tracking us the whole time—I made sure of it. And I knew that as soon as we came up here, as soon as we switched off the phones, he would believe that we were on the brink of going dark . . . that he would need to strike as soon as he possibly could.

"I wired the place up as soon as AA asked me for a safe house"—she gives the slightest hint of a smile before the gravity of the situation brings the sides of her mouth back down again . . . into a loping frown—"I thought it would be perfect. *Secluded*. The right place for us to take care of my . . ."

She chokes for a moment, and then sniffs. When she gets a hold on her emotions, she has a renewed steel in her eye, as if she has already cried all the tears over this situation—as if she has already been through all the heartbreak; and she just wants to get the explanation through with . . . wants to get the secrets out in the open.

". . . Take care of my father," Amy continues, "and his *group*." She gives another shake of her head. "Brian's exposed now—in terms of his physical defence; he was depending on my father to keep him safe, but he hasn't got that any longer."

Right as Amy wraps up this portion of her tale, one of the guards stirs.

On impulse, I reach for the handgun I snatched off one of them.

Point it at his head.

Before I can even draw my hand straight, Amy holds her arm out to me, as if her flesh and bone might be enough to stop the bullet. "*Anna!*" she says. "Wait! It's okay."

I don't lower the gun right away—there're still lingering suspicions, even though Amy has just confessed to us that she's wiped out her own father with a bomb . . . I guess that just flags up my own trust issues . . . with a *red* flag, no less.

When I meet Amy's eye, though, I do lower my gun.

The guard seems grateful too, his eyes sinking down from the barrel, to somewhere around my stomach.

"I paid them off," Amy says, then flips a glance in the direction of the guards. "I told them to be outside the cottage when the two of you were taken prisoner—and that they were to take you clear of the site." Another fleeting smile appears on, and then disappears from, Amy's lips. "Thankfully my dad demanded that you were taken clear—that part went smoothly."

The rising sob seems to come out of nowhere at all, like the swell rising up from beneath a wave. It grows up and out of Amy, arching her shoulders back, opening up her lungs. And then she blurts out a damp, flat, muffled *wail*.

I think quickly, lay the gun down—the one which I was previously holding on one of the guards—and then I throw my arm around Amy's shoulders.

She turns into me, shaking her head.

Her whole body trembling with sobs now.

As she realises just what she's done.

That she's killed her own father.

. . . And I thought *I* was cold-hearted.

She sobs away for five minutes or more, as I watch AA and Tabby over Amy's shoulder.

It's only as Amy's sobbing reaches its peak when I hear some words through it all.

"Anna . . . Anna?" Amy says.

"Yeah?" I say, cradling Amy in my arms, and feeling the blood welling out from the side of her head.

"The bomb . . . in your house . . . my dad . . . he made—he

had me set it there . . . there wasn't any other way to do it . . . and I made a mistake, did it on purpose . . . I didn't want to hurt anyone . . . I thought that a fire would be enough . . . be enough to make it seem like I *tried* . . . but my dad, he never . . . *never really* trusted me after that . . . but I used that trust against him . . . and it brought him here . . . it brought them *all* here."

As Amy collapses in my arms—apparently exhausted—I turn my attention back to the crumbling, burning cottage. And then back to us—to the *survivors*.

One thing's for certain, Amy's sacrifice won't be in vain.

Brian Mathewson must die.

Chapter Thirty-Three

I AT LEAST possess enough clarity of thought to phone ahead to Mark before turning up on his doorstep with a strange young woman in tow. He, of course, being the perfect boyfriend—or, well, *near-enough*, anyway—agrees to my request. No questions asked.

And, when me and Amy trudge in through the door of his home, he doesn't mention anything about AA's car . . . doesn't ask what became of the 'decent motor' AA turned up to the house in when he picked me up, and why he's suddenly arrived here in an estate car.

One of the many which Charlie Branwick's men left along the track leading up to the cottage.

Despite Amy's bump on the head, she made seriously short work of hotwiring it.

And we had no trouble on the trip down.

If I ever get around to buying a car, I might make a note of the model and see if there're any to be had . . . second-hand, of course . . . or, at the very least, an ex-display model.

I feel as if I can breathe again, just stepping into the hallway of Mark's home. And it feels even better to hear the gentle *rumble* of Tabby and AA driving off, away up the street—to give me and Amy a moment to put our feet up.

It now being a Wednesday night—time has been *really* weird these past few days—I'm sure that it looks several shades of odd to Mark that me and a 'work associate who recently lost her father' are turning up on his doorstep.

But, then again, he did say that we could use him as a 'base' .
. .

Realising that Amy's in a delicate condition, Mark gives me a helping hand, one of us on each side of her, helping her up the staircase. I guess that we're going to make good use of the twin beds in the guest room . . . if I don't finish harloting it up in Mark's bedroom later on—a *distinct* possibility.

Although Mark offers Amy a shower, she clearly hasn't the energy to accept—no matter how fluffy and inviting and *warmed* the towel is on the foot of her bed. But she does allow us—me specifically—to see to the wound on the side of her head.

Back up in Scotland, me and Tabby did a patching job. It wasn't the most pleasant task in the world to step back into that burned-out cottage of barbecued flesh, to search high and low for a first aid kit. But we did it.

What can I say?

The needs of the living outweigh those of the dead . . .

Now, though, looking at the bandages afresh, I can see that the blood's already soaked through the virgin-white gauze, turning it a rusty red-brown colour.

I glance back over my shoulder at Mark, as if he might be in some sort of position to offer me a secondary medical opinion. As if crafting wood might have something in common with stitching up wounds.

"Think she needs to go to A and E," Mark says.

I do too, but I don't say it—going to A and E would bring on too many questions.

My paranoia gets a little away from me, wondering if they have some kind of test, crossed-matched with recent incidents, to determine whether or not there might be a connection. All that information ready to hand over to the police.

To Brian Mathewson.

In the end, I content myself with a quick swab of the affected part of Amy's head, then, as if she's drifting apart from me, she lies herself down, closes her eyes and drifts off to sleep. That leaves me and Mark standing over her, in a creepy, almost pseudo-parental way.

"Sitting room?" Mark says, and I give him a nod.

As I bring the door shut behind me, I peer in through the narrowing crack, to Amy as she lies on her side, her back towards us. I watch on as her shoulders rise and arch back with her heavy breathing.

———

It being about ten o'clock at night, Nathan's already long-gone—headed up to bed, to get in whatever optimal amount of sleep teenagers are supposed to have every night before school.

And just saying that to myself I realise how me not knowing the answer, being the mother of a teenager and all, makes me out to be some sort of monster.

But, well, I suppose we've all got to be something.

I lean up against Mark's well-developed muscles on the sofa. It's one of those sofas which is *so* well loved that it's a little lumpy; a few scraps of beige stuffing stick out of burst seams in places. Mark, with his gentle craftsman's hands, trails his fingers through my hair. Lizzie arrives, hauls herself up onto the sofa and lies up against my stomach.

Almost without any movement, the TV blinks on.

Only then do I realise that Mark has the remote at all.

Mark flips through a few channels before finally settling on a talk show.

Already, just seeing the garish studio lighting, the overly camp host, with the tangerine skin and well-plucked eyebrows, sends a wave of nausea ploughing through my stomach. He has on a *very* tight-fitting, bright-blue suit with a scarlet tie. To my mind, he looks more like a fast-food chain restaurant owner than a TV presenter . . . but what do I know?

The show having just started, and the overly chirpy orchestral music still thrumming away in the background, I'm already not sure how much of this I can take. The host pitches up to a raised platform before the audience and begins to give his monologue. When the host makes a joke, I hear Mark give a slight chuckle above me . . . and his chuckle sends vibrations reverberating through my whole body.

Soothing.

Realising that I can do so without being discovered, I close my eyes, make the world go away for a while.

Almost like punctuation, Mark's body rumbles with laughter once a minute or so, and I settle in to just enjoying the sensation.

It's only when the presenter announces the first guest that I think to wrench an eyelid open:

Paula Stevenstar.

That name, it sounds familiar.

Through my bleary, single eye, I peer out at the screen, at the scantily dressed woman in her fifties tottering her way onto the stage; looking like, at any moment, she might topple right over on that pair of towering high heels and break her neck.

I take in the intricacies of her appearance.

The electric-pink cocktail dress she wears, and how to say that she has 'caked on' her makeup might well be putting the matter lightly.

She pulls off that trick which I've noted in older, more wrinkled—not to mention *self-conscious*—women.

She offers the presenter a kiss on his cheek, puckering her lips such a way so as not to move any other muscle on her face. As she pulls back from the presenter, I learn that he's called 'Harry', although I probably should've gathered as much from the backdrop of the show; the way there's a *huge* banner in the background declaring as much.

There's another fanfare from the out-of-sight orchestra and the presenter—*Harry*—places his hand in the small of Paula Stevenstar's back, guiding her over to a pair of turquoise sofas. He makes a mock bow once she's seated and Paula Stevenstar, again pulling that smile which doesn't affect a single muscle in her face, besides those in her lips, thanks him greatly.

The music fades down.

And Harry perches on the edge of his sofa, hands clasped together and appearing to be absolutely *enthralled* by his guest. Who am I to be cynical? For all I know, he *is* enthralled . . .

As Harry reels through the usual questions—asking her how she's been; and what she's been up to lately—Paula Stevenstar surely parrots the rote answers she's worked over with her legions of assistants. I wonder a little dizzily how many assistants she might've fired going into this show, for whatever reason. If there's one thing I've learned from being on the fringes of show business, it's that the talent *reigns* . . . and nothing may come between the Talent and the Show; not even an ever-so-slightly cold cup of coffee.

Harry quizzes Paula Stevenstar for the latest updates on her divorce—here she makes a joke about it being Lucky Seven, but I'm not totally sure if this doesn't go right over my head . . . because *seven* divorces, even for someone in show business, sounds far too many.

Or maybe I'm just an old traditional.

It's only when Harry stares right into the show cameras, shielding his eyes from the glare of the spotlights, screwing up his expression, that I feel my gut tighten. He seeks out somebody, jerks his head at them to come over, and then, the person off camera apparently acting coy, he jerks his head again—more vigorously this time.

Finally, the presenter—*Harry*—rises up off the sofa, and begins to clap.

Paula Stevenstar, too, seems somewhat beside herself, appearing almost to lose her mind, shaking her head, holding her hand up to cover her chuckling mouth.

The camera switches to a wide-angled shot, and I watch on as, from the side-lines, another man in a suit—this time a much more conservative charcoal shade—struts onto the scene.

Casually, he reaches out, allows Harry to give him a two-handed handshake; then the two of them retire to the sofa, alongside Paula Stevenstar.

It's only when Harry urges the man to sit down beside Paula that I get a proper read on the face.

That my brain manages to *finally* click into place.

And I realise that it's Brian Mathewson.

That he must be the person representing Paula Stevenstar.

I *knew* that name was familiar.

My whole body stiffens all of a sudden.

Lizzie gives me a *brurr* of protest, and then, apparently not getting the tranquil sleep that she was inspecting, she hoiks herself off the sofa, down onto the carpet—obviously hauling herself off to some other *quieter* nook or cranny about Mark's house where a cat can get her twenty-three hours of sleep uninterrupted.

When Mark reacts, glances down at me, and with his gentle hand draws back my fringe to look at my face, he says, "Did you fall asleep?"

My mind quickly locks onto Mark's assumption—that he believes the twitch I just gave was a result of me falling down in my dreams; something like that. And not seeing any other way of passing off my reaction, I manage to get out a muted, ". . . Yeah."

"You can go up to bed if you like," he says. "No need for you to be polite, or anything—I'll be heading up in a minute or so."

As Mark's words tumble about my brain, I turn my attention back to the screen, and to Brian Mathewson sitting there, on the sofa, chuckling it up with Harry and Paula Stevenstar.

I wonder if they know just how powerful Brian Mathewson really is.

That, if he really wanted to, he could have both of them killed.

And get away with it.

Or—at the very least—Brian Mathewson would *believe* he would get away with it.

Which only makes him all the more dangerous.

Chapter Thirty-Four

WHEN I WAKE UP in the morning, in the bed alongside Amy, I instinctively turn to look at her face, to see how her head wound is getting on.

But she's not there.

My heart rattles about my ribcage, beating frantically for several seconds. It takes me a couple of deep breaths to get it back under control. I wonder if she might've snuck out in the middle of the night, got away from me before I could ask any more questions.

In all honesty, I'm not sure that I could have too many complaints.

After all, Amy has already contributed more than enough to the Demise of Brian Mathewson.

She has killed her own father.

However, I hear the footsteps out on the landing, and when I turn my head to look, it's to observe Amy, wrapped up in a towel, rounding the doorframe. She has another, smaller, towel wrapped about her blond hair.

My eyes instinctively drift to the side of Amy's face, and to the wound.

I see that the blood has all dried now, leaving it a brownie-red colour.

She meets my eye with her sapphire-blues and gives me a faint smile. "Morning," she says. "Funny that we've seemed to end up sharing bedrooms during this whole ordeal, isn't it?"

I give Amy some privacy, turning my back on her while she dries herself off and gets dressed.

I busy myself with organising my clothes, the clothes that're all still arranged around me in plastic bags.

I shake my head, more than a couple of times, at the purchases that me and AA made.

I know—to the fullest degree—that several of the items; notably a glittery bikini, and a pair of ruby-red hot pants; never would've made it into my shopping basket if not for his presence. I make a mental note that the next time I need to go on a survival shopping spree that I'll leave AA at home, or at whatever place will accept children at such short notice . . .

"Anna?" Amy says, from behind me.

I turn to look, see that she's now wearing a pair of blue jeans, an understated plain white t-shirt over the top. The smaller towel still wrapped around her hair. She drops her voice down so that it nears a whisper. "Have you got it?" She stalks a few paces closer to me, as if 'the walls have ears'. "Have you got it *here*?"

I think about the Death Log, and although I probably could quite easily utter some lie to Amy, about how I—*really*—have no idea where I might've misplaced it, my reflexes betray me.

The question has hardly left Amy's lips when I feel my gaze drifting over to the bookshelf, and then, without hesitation, lingering over the book behind which I stashed the memory stick. Amy follows my gaze, then pads on over to the spot. She extends a bony finger to point at the book which—all of a sudden—has become the very centre of my attention. "Is it here?" she says.

I suppose that I should be being nice to Amy, so I think only to give a firm nod.

Without wasting time, Amy yanks the book out from its slot on the shelf. She inspects the cover for a moment and then realises that it's coated in dust. She gives a subtle grimace, lays the book down on top of the bookcase and then wipes her hands on her jean pockets. Then she crouches down and inspects the gap left behind.

She prods her fingers in through the hole and retrieves the memory stick—the *Death Log*—from within. She holds it up to the light, as if she has just uncovered some long-lost relic, before glancing to me. "This is it?" she says.

I nod back at her.

She nods to me.

And then, without another word, she replaces the Death Log back where she drew it out from, blocking it back into its hiding place with the dusty book.

That done, she treads back over to the other twin bed, where she was getting dressed. She looks out of the window, and down into the street, drying her hair with the smaller towel now. Her blond hair is much longer than I first thought, and I remind myself that, throughout the whole of this episode, she has kept it up in either a ponytail or a bun.

Her eyes twitch back and forth as she surveys the road outside.

Then, without warning, she turns back to me and says, "Are we expecting AA?"

Chapter Thirty-Five

ALTHOUGH I CAN'T quite explain what it was that I expected—that AA would leave me and Amy alone for a week or so so that we might have a chance to recover?—I find myself balling my fingers into fists as I descend the stairs.

An inexplicable, and unexpected, anger flashes right through me.

Only when I've jammed the latch on the front door down and crossed over the threshold, do I realise that I'm still in my pyjamas—the pair of tracksuit bottoms and the baggy t-shirt. When the bare soles of my feet meet with the scouring brush-textured doormat, and then with the frosted gravel, I hardly even register the pain.

My eyes remain fixed on the estate car, pulled up to the curb, outside Mark's house, the exhaust drooling out a steady stream of grey-black smoke. As I draw closer to the car, I expect AA to catch sight of me—or, more precisely, the thunderous expression on my face—and take off along the road at a rapid click. But, no. He remains parked up, in that purloined car of his.

When I reach the driver's window, I rap my knuckles against it.

There's a flurry of activity from within which—surely—attests that AA wasn't paying all that much attention to persons approaching his car.

AA rapidly winds down the window, turns to look at me. His eyes are webbed with red veins and those dark circles are back again, clinging to the bases of his eye sockets. I can tell that it's been something of a long night for him . . . perhaps he's spent the night in the car itself.

"What the hell are you doing here?" I say, through gritted teeth, and hardly able to control myself.

AA stares at me—long and hard—as if he's attempting to divine some long-concealed truth, as if he's having trouble with the semantics of my words. "I couldn't exactly call you up, now, could—?"

I cut him off. "You turn up here, outside the house, in that *stolen* car?" I shake my head vigorously. "Are you not aware that, by now, the entirety of the British police force is most likely doing its very best to track it?"

AA stares back at me once more—his eyes widening as if he's only now realising this fear. When he speaks, I'm surprised that he manages to keep his tone so calm; his voice from cracking about the edges. "Brian knows, Anna," he says.

I look at AA for several moments, just processing what he said.

Then I say, "And how does that change anything?"

AA gives a shake of his head and then looks out over the top of the steering column, to the quiet mid-morning road out in front of him. "It means that he'll be coming for you, Anna—he'll be coming for *all* of us."

"He doesn't know I'm here," I fire back.

"Maybe not, but he will do soon."

I feel a tightness grip my stomach. My heart flutters up to my throat.

I swallow it back down.

"It doesn't matter," I say. "It doesn't change anything."

AA taps his fingers against the ruts in the plastic steering wheel. "So we go ahead with the plan—as we agreed it?" He turns back to me then, stares into my eyes, and I see—for the first time I can recall—that he's *worried*.

"Yes," I say, "there's no turning back any more—we have to finish what we started." I tilt my head back to indicate Mark's house over my shoulder. "Amy didn't firebomb her father's cottage—and her dad *with it*—just so that we could back out at the last minute."

"When?" AA says, turning to face forwards again, as if he's about to put his foot down, speed off and away from the house.

"Tonight," I say, and then step away from AA's car, knowing that—for all my posturing; all my brave words—there really *isn't* any turning back now.

Chapter Thirty-Six

I HELP AMY to some breakfast and then sort of lurk around the spare room, trying to draw my thoughts straight. It feels like I'll be in dire need of a holiday once all of this is over . . . if I'm still *alive*, that is . . . I wonder if there's anybody on the planet who lives such a tangled life as I do—so many comings; so many goings . . . though mostly *goings*.

Realising that I'm acting sort of neurotic, I decide to set my mind to putting together my wardrobe for the evening—for Brian Mathewson's long-awaited demise.

All black, of course, anything else would be a departure from the norm.

Just like the other days I've spent at Mark's house, the rhythm is fairly consistent.

I go about my day; while Mark goes about his.

Off in his workshop, crafting his masterpieces, in his own world.

And with no idea of all that's taking place around him.

So close, and yet *far* out of his reach.

It's about four in the afternoon, with Nathan back home from school, when I peer out of the guest-room window and notice the white van—sort of like a *builder's van*—pulling up outside the house, drawing into the curb.

I examine a woman in a wide-brimmed, straw hat getting down from the cab. Alongside her are a pair of men who could—quite easily; from their stature—be builders. Except that they're wearing suits. Perhaps they have more in keeping with bodyguards.

I watch on as they crunch their way across the gravel drive-way, and up to the front door.

I peer down on the woman, dressed in a long, beige jacket which sweeps about her ankles. She has on a pair of sunglasses, too; and holds her hands in her pockets as she awaits the answer to the doorbell.

Amy ducks into the guest room, returning from the bath-room. She gives me a scowl and, being a good girl, arrives at my side without uttering a word—not wanting to break my concentration. She meets my gaze and looks down on the assembled group on the doorstep too. Neither one of us needs to say what we're thinking . . . not only does this trio appear suspicious, but the woman seems familiar, too.

Time for me and Amy to sit back and play that we're not at home.

Still watching the front door, I hear Mark's heavy footsteps, a couple of coughs, as he enters the hallway below us. I listen for the percussive, slightly metallic *thud* as he releases the door latch. "Yes?" he says, his voice echoing up the stairs and along the land-ing, passing in through the guest-room doorway.

"Mr Rawler?" the woman says, her voice clean and crisp.

And more familiar than ever now.

Perhaps this is Brian's plan—perhaps he wants to get me and Amy right now; *here*, in an innocent bystander's home.

I look to Amy, and, without any sort of gesture, she stalks across the room, taking extreme care not to make so much as a sound with her footsteps. She digs about within one of the plastic bags, produces a gun—one for each of us.

If Brian is going to try and finish this right here and now, we're going to be taking his henchmen down with him.

Silently, I look over the gun in my hand—nothing more than a 9mm, but enough to do the job if it comes down to it.

I turn my attention back to the conversation happening below—to the woman's words.

"We're from Child Protection," she says, "and we've received a report that you may be illegally harbouring somebody else's child on the premises."

There's the *rustle* of paper, and I imagine her slitting open a brown envelope to reveal a page within.

Silence rings out through the house as Mark—apparently—reads the paper.

"What is this?" Mark says.

"It's what it looks like, Mr Rawler—we have permission to search the premises, to see if there is any truth to the claims specified by this order."

My heart stops beating.

I turn to Amy, see that her expression is just as vacant as my own.

It would be so much simpler if they had drawn a gun.

If they had ordered—*demanded*—that Mark go with them.

But that's not what's happened.

I listen to Mark's response.

"I spoke, on the phone, I sent off the form you asked for. Next Day Delivery. I got notification that you received it."

"Falsified document, Mr Rawler," the woman replies. "I'm afraid that it is in no way valid."

"But . . . but," I hear Mark jabber out in reply.

"If you'll excuse us, Mr Rawler, I'd like to get this over with as quickly as possible."

From downstairs, there's another bout of silence.

I imagine Mark shaking his head at the page still, trying to fathom what's going on.

And then, "Mr Rawler?"

When Mark speaks again, his voice is flat—*toneless*—and I just about make him out, mumbling, "Come in, then, I suppose."

With a series of smart footsteps, I hear the men tread into the front hall, accompanied by the less-determined twin *clack* of the woman's high heels. I look to Amy, and she looks back to me.

We both stash our guns under the sheets, sit on the edge of one of the beds, and wait for the men to stamp their way up the staircase.

"I'm sorry about this, Mr Rawler, really I am," the woman says, back down in the hall, "but sometimes there's no other way to do these things." She pauses, ostensibly to draw a deep breath. "If you wouldn't mind, I have some paperwork for you to sign."

Mark mutters something else under his breath—something which sounds like a swearword, but since the woman doesn't ask that Mark repeat himself, the word goes without clarification.

The footsteps on the staircase get louder.

I take in one of the suited men, looking like an ape dressed for a birthday party; the other one looks much the same, but with ginger hair instead of brown.

As the men pass by the guest room, they look in on me and

Amy, but they don't react at all. They continue on along the landing—on a beeline to Nathan's bedroom. I grit my teeth, wishing that there was something I could do . . . if this had something to do with Brian, if these men had been sent by Brian to get me and Amy, then there would be any of a million things for me to do. As it is, though, I can only sit back and watch.

Observe law and order taking place.

One of the men delivers a sharp pair of knocks to Nathan's bedroom door, before getting an affirmative answer and stepping inside.

I perch on the edge of the mattress, prone, ready to act.

In a heightened sense of mind.

Ready to pull off my Supergirl act . . . whatever that entails.

The screaming begins soon after I hear the footsteps cross the threshold; enter into Nathan's bedroom. Only this time it's not because of Nathan's night terrors.

I sink my fingernails into the heel of my hand, then bite down hard on my tongue.

Nothing you can do, Anna—there's nothing you can do.

I watch on as the pair of men lug Nathan, still dressed in his frog-green school uniform, past the door of the guest room. Each of the men holding tight to one of Nathan's arms.

Nathan aims kicks at the men and, much to my delight, catches one of them in his calf muscle.

The afflicted man gives a grunt and squashes his features together.

I watch on as the man gives Nathan a stern look, and—apparently, if Nathan's screams are anything to go by—tightens his hold severely.

Maybe it's watching Nathan disappear down the staircase which does it. Maybe it's the knowledge that it could—*quite easily*

—be my own son, Ben, that I'm watching being carried away by strangers, but it's then that I lift myself out of inaction.

I launch myself off the bed, hurl myself through the doorway and out onto the landing.

My feet hardly touch the ground as I take the steps two and three at a time, headed for the front hall. On my heels, I can hear Amy calling out after me.

I see the group of them before me—in the front hall—I spot Mark, lurking back, clinging to that piece of paper in his hand, squeezing it so tightly that he's creased it. The woman beside him, watching on, her bloodless lips the only aspect of her face visible beneath her straw hat. The two heavy-set men in suits, with the violently protesting Nathan between them, have their backs to me.

They're ready to leave through the open doorway.

To the van outside.

My mind doesn't allow me any more conscious thoughts.

I leap off the staircase, with still four or five stairs to go, and aim myself at a point between one of the men's shoulder blades.

When I make contact, it's like my fists pound into a brick wall, but I can feel myself falling down.

Can feel the man falling down beneath me.

And—all the time—Nathan's screaming.

Almost the second that the world comes to a halt, with me kneeling on top of the downed man, I feel a strong arm take hold of me. And I know, right away, feeling those calloused, sausage-like fingers pinching my skin, that I won't be able to resist.

There's no way that I can put up a fight.

Not against this sort of brute strength.

But, almost as soon as the fingers have made contact with my skin, I feel them give way once more. I'm free again.

I jerk my head upwards, trying to bring some sort of sense back to the scene. To quieten the pounding of my heart in my eardrums.

I catch sight of Amy, somehow having thrown herself up on top of the other man's shoulders.

Nathan now, I see, stands off to one side, having been forgotten.

He gapes at the scene.

It's then—seemingly out of nowhere—that his eyes lock onto mine, and I somehow have the presence of mind to mouth to him, *Run!*

He stands stock-still, continuing to be stunned by the scene playing out in the front hall of his home, but then he seems to absorb my words at last.

He widens his eyes—flares his nostrils.

Then bolts out through the open door.

Across the gravel driveway.

Escaping.

The bulky man beneath me, apparently having noticed the refugee, calls out to his companion.

But his companion continues to be somewhat busy with Amy, up on his shoulders.

I keep up my strength, hold all my weight down on the man beneath me, until I observe Nathan turn the corner, and sprint away, off up the street.

Then I can't hold on any longer.

It's taken all my strength to pin this huge man beneath me.

To the hall floor.

With a *groan* the man hauls me off him.

I land with a *bump* on the staircase; my limbs sprawled about me.

All of a sudden, I feel the man standing over me, blocking out the sunlight which flows in through the open door. The man grinds his jaw and raises his fist, over his shoulder, ready to bring it down.

Maybe it's fear—maybe it's *exhaustion*—but I close my eyes.

And I wait for the blackness.

Almost embrace it.

But it doesn't come.

Only when I feel my heart trundle on another few beats, do I allow myself to open my eyes again, and to see Mark there, gripping tight to the man's arm, preventing him from swinging his fist through the air; putting me into a restless sleep.

The man struggles briefly with Mark, but then, with a hurried glance to the woman in the beige coat, gives up. When it becomes apparent that the man's not going to cause me any sort of physical harm, Mark backs off, releases him from his hold.

I look to Amy, who is also back on the ground.

She stands a little way back from her own ape in a suit, scowling at the scene.

The woman nods to the men. "Run him down," she says. "He won't have gone far."

Alarmed by this, I turn to Mark, expect him to say something.

But Mark's expression remains neutral. He looks to me and Amy, then says, "Let them take him in—they're right, the papers *are* falsified."

I feel something approaching exasperation.

I shoot a glance at Amy.

She looks back at me.

Everything within me wants to grab those men again—stop them from getting hold of Nathan.

But what am I supposed to do?

If Mark says that they need to take Nathan?

For the first time I look to the woman, who busies herself with Mark, handing him another stack of papers. "You need to return the forms to the specified address by the written date." She tips the brim of her hat to Mark and then ventures out through the doorway.

It's only when I catch sight of her face in profile that a feeling stirs at the base of my gut.

I realise that I have seen this woman before.

I catch sight of her blond hair, kept orderly beneath her hat. And then I breathe in that unusual mixture of blackberries and hazelnuts.

The blond woman.

The woman who met with me and AA before we took up the job for Brian—*Hell Bird*—which saw us flying out to that island.

I want to reach out, grab her by the elbow, but I remain frozen, sitting on the staircase.

Knowing that I need to let her go.

That I need to let *all* of this go.

But, as the front door slams shut behind the blond woman, and her pair of apes, I can't shift the feeling that Brian has all of us—but *me* especially—right behind the white ball.

And he's ready to strike.

Chapter Thirty-Seven

A S NIGHT SETTLES IN, I have to admit that I really
have no idea what's going to happen next. I remind
myself I told AA that we're going to be taking down Brian Mathewson tonight—that this *all* ends tonight.

And yet, I can hardly summon the strength to stitch even a
pair of thoughts together.

Although I try to speak with Mark—to see how he's feeling—
he's despondent, and he shuts himself off in his workshop,
putting his blood, sweat and—no doubt—*tears* into his work.

So that nobody else will see.

I sit on the floor of the guest room, my back pressed hard
against the bedframe.

I try to sift through my thoughts—through everything that's
happened.

Trying to get things into their right order.

I think about how Amy was responsible for the start of all
this; how she blamed me for the death of Grendelin. If it hadn't

been for her then maybe—*just maybe*—Brian really would've let me go.

Charlie Branwick wouldn't have put a kill order out on me.

Then there was my house burning down, and losing everything—what little I *did* possess.

I can't help wondering about those phone calls, the ones which Mark received from the Adoption Agency, or whoever was calling him up. Was that Brian all along? Was that Brian himself on the phone, speaking to Mark?

Did Brian know that Mark's paperwork for him adopting Nathan wasn't one-hundred-per-cent authentic?

. . . Or did he—*somehow*—manufacture that out of nowhere?

And have Mark believe him?

I don't suppose I'll get the answer from just sitting here.

There's only one person who can answer these questions for me—and only one person who, in the past few weeks, at least, can be held responsible for making my life a misery.

It all comes from one place:

Mathewson Media.

I look to Amy, knowing that she must be suffering through some extreme mental trauma herself.

For the duration of the evening—ever since the apes in suits and the blond woman left—she's been huddled up on the other bed, reading a book.

Her role in the Plan is very much through with.

I recall the conversation we had back up in the cottage—in Scotland—about how she had some sort of masterplan to take care of her father, and—just as importantly—the entire network he ran about the country.

Keeping Brian safe.

Watching Brian's back.

I wonder what Brian was thinking, taking away Mark's son.

Is this his attempt at hurting me?

By hurting those around me?

I draw another breath, and I think about my own family—my children; Josie and Ben. And I know, before I go through with the Plan that I'm going to have to go and see them.

As I rise up from the floor, set about putting on my black clothing—so that I can better meld with the shadows; with the night—Amy stirs from the other bed.

She peers up over her book at me. "Are you going?" she says.

I dig about for that gun I stashed beneath my bedsheets—recover it—and then look to her.

"You don't have a holster by any chance, do you?"

Chapter Thirty-Eight

I STAND OUTSIDE my ex-husband Arnold's house.

For the longest time, I stare at its silhouette, growing up and out of the pristine front garden: the garden which, Arnold's new partner—*Kate*—keeps in perfect condition.

Whenever I've tried to make anything grow, it either withers away and dies; or else, as in the case of the bushes in the back garden of my former home, it takes on a life of itself . . . completely unable to be controlled.

I think about knocking on the door, and then I think about the awkward conversation with Arnold or—*God forbid*—Kate that will follow.

How they'll make that subtle point about how I'm *supposed* to call before 'dropping by'; and how, in any case, it's already gone ten o'clock at night and the kids have school tomorrow.

That they're already sleeping.

And so, with that thought on my mind, I decide it's best to bypass the front door all together.

I glance about the quiet street, to the drawn curtains, and the warm, orange lights which emanate from within. Those little scenes send a thrill through my gut—making me wonder why *I* can't be inside one of those houses; why I can't be toasting my feet by an open fire, watching crap on television, laughing to myself.

And then I remember my job.

And my employer.

That's the reason.

That's the reason *why*.

I turn my attention back to the house before me, and eye up the garage roof.

Decision made, I hop over the low, brick garden wall, onto the soft, grassy front lawn of Arnold's house. I take hold of the steel drainpipe and haul myself up the wall, lug my weight up onto the roof. I guess not having eaten properly for the past few hours has had some benefits. There's not all that much of me to lug upwards.

Once on the roof of the garage, and feeling that the tiles aren't exactly completely stable, I eye up the house itself.

It must be the adrenalin which floods through my veins; which sends the thrill right down to my gut, because no part of my logical brain participates in the action of hurling myself across the gap.

When I land, my foot causes a loose roof tile to grate against another.

I hold my breath, and then, in horror, watch in the semi-darkness as the tile slides free from its place on the roof, and then slips away.

I shut my eyes, as if that's going to help with making the

sound of the tile landing on the tarmacked drive below any quieter.

It shatters with an almost ear-splitting *smash.*

A sound that the entire street has *surely* heard.

My breathing quickens. My heart thuds in my ears.

And I know that I have to get going—that I can't just linger here, in plain sight.

As I scrabble across the roof tiles, still trying to make my step as quiet as possible, not wanting to attract more attention than is entirely necessary, I hear the front door, directly below, open with a *creak.*

I reach the roof window, the one which looks down into the landing of the upper floor of the house. I stick my fingernails in about the edges and—*sure enough*—I feel it give beneath my grip.

Thank God for Arnold's sloppiness . . . his lack of waterproof security about the place.

I open the window wide enough so that I'll be able to pass through, and then, before I squeeze myself inside, I glance back over my shoulder. Out to the street behind me.

No neighbours have emerged from their homes.

I'm in luck . . . or so it seems.

Down below, I hear Arnold and Kate's hushed voices. No doubt they're going to inspect the damage. I overhear Arnold's voice as he—*apparently*—discovers the shattered tile.

"Bloody cats," he says.

And then I slip in through the rooftop window.

Undetected.

Chapter Thirty-Nine

THE HOUSE is totally silent upstairs.

A light shines brightly above my head.

That's for my daughter Josie's benefit.

She's scared of the dark . . . or—at least—she was the last time that I spoke to her.

I stalk along the landing, listening for any sound below. It's not until I've reached the door to Josie's room that I hear the voices returning through the front door, the door shutting with a *slam* behind them.

I stand still, not wanting to make a sound for the next few seconds.

I wait for the voices.

They start speaking again—their tones too low for me to make out.

But I can tell that they're headed for the kitchen.

Away from me.

I take a deep breath and then reach out to prod Josie's door open a little more. She already has it left open a good few centimetres so that the light from the landing will be able to get inside.

So that she won't be left in darkness.

I glance back over my shoulder, for some reason believing that somebody's watching me.

Nobody is.

And so I steal inside.

————

Josie's bedroom, as always, smells strongly of soap.

Through the darkness, beyond the toys scattered all over the floor, I can make out Josie's slumped-up form in bed, beneath a duvet. She has her back to me. As I creep closer, she stirs in her sleep, and then, without announcement, turns about to face me.

I can just about make out the black dots of her eyes in the gloom.

She squints at me. "Mummy?" she says, in a voice which is too loud.

Which will *surely* be overheard by Arnold and Kate downstairs.

I listen out for their voices, for any sign that they might have noticed . . . and then, because I've always been a pessimist, I tune my attention to the sound of approaching sirens.

I can't hear any.

Yet.

I come closer still.

Josie rubs at her eyes with her fists, and then says, "Mummy Anna?" She gives a wide yawn before sitting up straight in bed. "I thought that you were Mummy Kate."

I feel a burn pass through my gut to hear Josie refer to Kate as any sort of 'Mummy'. But then I snap to my senses. I only have myself to blame for having blurred—*outright confused*—my children's parental roles.

Without saying anything in reply, I go to Josie's side, sit on the edge of her mattress. Then, with her eyes wide, looking through the darkness at me, I reach out and brush back her hair from her face. It makes me want to cry—knowing that I might not be coming back from tonight; that it's going to be Brian Mathewson or me.

A zero-sum game.

Although I can feel the tears welling in the corners of my eyes, I force them back down, tell myself that I can't let anything happen to my daughter. That she doesn't deserve to have me crumble before her as her parting memory of me.

So I reach out for her hand, give it a squeeze, and then lean forward to give her a kiss on the forehead. "Lie down, darling," I say, "it's bedtime."

Josie gives me a smile and does as I tell her.

Soon enough, she's lying flat on the bed, her duvet drawn up over her.

Breathing heavily.

Without another word, I release her hand and go to see Ben.

———

I step past the screwed-up clothes all over the floor, and I note how the air reeks of deodorant; though there's not yet that musky scent of man. I suppose that all the boys at school have started using deodorant, so Ben—by osmosis—has decided to as well.

Ben, like Josie, remains beneath his duvet, but, unlike Josie, he doesn't wake up from his sleep as I lean forward and plant a kiss on his forehead.

He moves about in his sleep, screwing up his features before turning over on his side to face the wall.

And then I steal my way back out of his bedroom.

Almost smashing my face up against the tip of Arnold's nose.

Chapter Forty

ARNOLD'S SABLE EYES. His light-brown hair shaved back to stubble. Then his parted lips.

I have no idea if he's going to cry out for help, if he's going to 'raise the alarm', but before waiting long enough to find out, I reach out and press my hand over his mouth.

He doesn't struggle against me and I decide that I'm fairly safe in letting him go.

When I do, he opens his eyes wide, his whole face sketched with shock.

"Anna," he says, his voice a husky whisper. "What . . ."

I cut him off with a shake of my head. "I'm sorry," I say, keeping my voice at the level of a whisper as I reply, "I know I should've called; I know that I should've knocked on the door, but . . . *tonight*, this could be . . . I don't know . . . the *end?*"

Why the last part of my speech comes out as a question, I really have no idea.

But there it is.

Arnold wrinkles his eyebrows together. "What're you talking about?" he says, and I'm only too aware of his eyes drifting down to my thigh, to where I have my gun holstered.

I didn't have enough presence of mind to stash it somewhere —under a bush, perhaps—before breaking into the house. I didn't anticipate being discovered, either.

Arnold looks up at me with alarm in his eyes now. "Anna," he says. "What's going on?"

"It's okay," I reply, surprised to find a smile stitching back my lips. "It might well be over after tonight, you won't have to ever lay eyes on me again—won't that be pleasant?"

Arnold starts to shake his head and then seems to catch himself as he appears to absorb the words, as he extracts meaning from them. "Anna, please . . ." he begins, and then his voice gets dry all of a sudden, his throat appears to constrict ". . . I *love* you."

My heart bumps a few times.

Even though I know it to be true—have always *assumed* that it's true . . . even now, after all this time—I can't help but feel a touch taken back to hear it now.

At this most emotionally charged of moments.

I turn my attention to any sound from downstairs, any sign that Kate might be coming. That's something which I don't think I'd be able to cope with. Sure, maybe I've already screwed up my own life, but that doesn't mean I'm going to screw up Arnold's— having him running about at all hours with his ex-wife.

I look back to Arnold, lean forwards and plant a kiss on his cheek. His cheek is a little scratchy from stubble, and I get the feeling he hasn't shaved for a good few days . . . maybe he's trying to grow a beard; God forbid. "Goodbye," I say, and then turn away from him.

But, before I can turn my back, I feel his firm grip on my shoulder. He has the strength to spin me back around to face him. A physical strength that I never would've believed he possessed until now.

"Annie," he says, looking me in the eye again. "Please just tell me what's happening—what you're involved with." He stares firmly into my eyes. "Is it *drugs?*" His voice becomes a gruff whisper when he mentions *that* word . . .

"No," I say, "it's not drugs."

"Then *what?*" Arnold says, his eyes almost bulging from their sockets.

I begin to shake my head, and then I wonder, if this all ends tonight—if one of us; me or Brian, is going down—then what could it hurt to tell him the truth.

I guess that I can only *try*.

Decided, I look back to Arnold. "Don't flip out about this or anything, okay?"

Arnold just looks back at me with a wide-eyed stare, waiting for me to fill him in on the details. His eyes dive down once more to the gun holstered at my thigh.

And I do my very best to explain.

"I don't know what you thought of me—if you believed I was *unemployed*, or what. Anyway, I suppose you could say that, over these past few years, I've been working freelance. Been paying the bills under my own steam." I pause for a second. "Well, with a little help from a client, that is."

Arnold furrows his brow, gives a slight shake of his head. "I'm sorry, Anna," he says, his voice still down at a whisper—like mine. "I really don't follow."

"Okay," I say, holding up my hand. "When you thought I was unemployed, or whatever, the truth is that I've been killing people"—my breath comes shallow here, and my voice drops down another level so that it's almost below a whisper —"*for money.*"

I don't know quite what to expect in the way of a reaction from Arnold.

Maybe I think that he's going to balk at this, puff out his cheeks, roll his eyes. Or else, perhaps I imagine that he's going to crumple at the knees, sink down to the ground, break out into some panicky fit as if what I've just told him is something he suspected all along but hasn't quite been able to believe.

Until now.

Instead, though, Arnold's eyes just drift away from mine, reach for a spot in mid-air just above my head. As I stand there, in the silence of the landing, though, I notice that he begins— steady, slow and sure—to nod his head in response. As if an understanding *is* dawning on him.

"Anna . . ." he utters from his dried lips, but adds nothing else.

I reach up, give him a tender touch on the cheek, and then say, once again, and perhaps for the last time, "Goodbye."

And I leave him there; equal parts beleaguered, stunned and resigned.

Chapter Forty-One

OUTSIDE, the chill in the air surprises me.

I suppose it's because of the difference between the warm, centrally-heated air of the house and Mother Nature's winter. We humans are good at keeping out the cold.

I shuffle myself over to the edge of the garage roof, stare at my legs dangling down, and see the concrete slabs just below. And then, with a quick word of courage, I implore myself to drop.

When I land, I bend my knees.

As I head out of the driveway, and away from Arnold and my children's house—away from *Kate's* house—I half expect Arnold to arrive in the doorway, and to call out to me, for him to *beg* me not to leave . . . to stay with him, to 'get help'.

Striding along the pavement, heading away from the house at a rapid click, I can't help but wonder if Arnold believed my story —or if, right now, he's in the process of getting me sectioned.

Perhaps that's all that can save me now:

The Men in White Coats.

I quicken my pace, already sketching the route in my mind, already thinking through my plan. I'll catch a taxi, from the rank a little way up ahead. I'll ask the driver to cart me over to Mathewson Media, where I *know* Brian will be waiting.

Then it'll all be over.

As I turn the corner, I'm dimly aware of a car engine over my shoulder. I can hear it finding a low gear. The vibrations from its engine rumble through the pavement, and up through the soles of my trainers. I try to put it out of my mind.

But the engine sound only grows louder.

Until I can feel the car trundling along beside me.

I hear the electronic *whine* of a window winding down.

Already scolding myself for paying attention—no doubt some construction-site foreman looking for some late-night female *thrills*—I turn my head to look.

And, staring out of the window, I see AA's face. "Don't tell me you're going to bloody *walk* the whole way there."

My eyes linger over the car.

A sleek estate car.

At first I pin it as being the same car which we swiped from up in Scotland; one of Charlie Branwick's which we travelled back down here in; and which AA seems to have found a certain preference for.

But then I take a second glance, realise that it's not the one we travelled down in. And that it has more in common—to my long-suffering eye—with a vehicle from Brian Mathewson's carpool.

Despite AA's words, I *do* keep on walking for another few paces.

And then I catch onto the idiocy of it all.

A *taxi.*

Those things have surveillance cameras these days, and who knows what else?

And me, here, walking about town with a gun strapped to my thigh as if Great Britain was some kind of rogue state.

Although the logical part of my brain takes over, I don't turn right away, accept AA's offer. Maybe I believe that I can do it all for myself—perhaps I *think* that, up until now, I've really done this all on my own. That I really have been a 'freelancer' all along.

When the truth is wildly different.

I come to a halt.

And get in the car.

———

As I sit in the passenger seat, I reflect on AA's current motor.

How it's a detergent-coloured, green-blue, two-door hatchback.

The seats are a fairly unpleasant plasticky material which makes a *zip* noise when I try to haul myself upright. And I continually feel as if I'm sliding down the seat, gradually slipping down into the floor space. The air smells strongly of neutral, new-car smell fragrance.

I've hardly sat my bottom down on the seat when AA offers me a mint, 'to put my mind at ease', and I accept his offer.

Peppermint.

At least I'll be meeting Brian with fresh breath.

As AA drives me along, he appears serious—at least in profile —utterly absorbed by driving us straight along the road, as if it's his job, and his job alone, to ensure that I get to Mathewson Media; that I don't attempt to shirk my responsibility.

Just like always, it seems, AA is sharply dressed in a pitch-black, well-tailored suit; and I can't help wondering if he has a specific part of his household budget he puts aside for purchasing new suits, or if he simply has such an enormous stockpile of suits that he never needs to wear the same one twice.

As we drive along in AA's *latest* vehicular acquisition, I say, "How'd you know that I'd be around here?"

AA sniffs a laugh and then turns the corner sharply.

The motion of the car sends me rocking into the door.

I settle myself back upright.

"You're not too hard to predict," AA says.

"I'm not, huh?" I shoot back, already feeling a touch slighted by the implication of this comment.

AA shakes his head, and continues to drive us on through the streets; away from my children, and Arnold, forever. "You know, Anna," AA says, "you're probably the closest thing I have to a best friend—and I take extreme pride in knowing, at all times, exactly what my friends are thinking."

"So what am I thinking about now?"

AA shrugs his shoulders, gives a slight smile and then slips me a sidelong glance. "I didn't say that I'm a *mind reader*, Anna, only that I know what's going on in that brain of yours—what sort of behaviour you're most likely to exhibit."

I think long and hard about reaching over, grabbing hold of the steering wheel and jerking the car off the road. I wonder if AA would see *that* coming?

But I resist the temptation.

There're greater evils that arrogance at work here.

And his name is Brian Mathewson.

We drive the rest of the journey in silence, only the gentle, *hairdryer-like* hum of the car's engine. I can hardly believe it when the great, glassy mausoleum that is Mathewson Media grows up and out of the pavement before us.

Up high in the building, I can spot the reflection of the moon.

Tonight's a clear night.

A *cold* night.

Without another word, AA turns the car down a side alley, one which, during the day, I suppose is used for supply vehicles. For those smaller vans supplying the Mathewson Media cafeteria with its always delicious, *luxurious* food . . . other vans supplying toilet paper and bottles of disinfectant . . . and now this side alley is used to help sneak in me—*an assassin.*

When I glance back to AA, waiting for him to tell me what to do next, or perhaps only looking for some sort of emotional support, he merely points beyond me; through the passenger window of the car; to the alley outside.

The light is murky, of course. The single light which illuminates the side alley is located a long way from us; back near the main road. So when I stare out through the window, into the surrounding plastic, flip-lid dumpsters, it takes my brain a few moments to fully process the gloom—to project some sort of sense onto it.

But I can see a figure.

Standing there.

In the shadows.

Finally, my brain twigs.

Works out just who it is.

By now I should know that redhead anywhere.

Tabby.

Chapter Forty-Two

I LEAVE AA BEHIND, perhaps not treating what might well be our last ever encounter with the respect it deserves. When I emerge into the frosty air of the side alley outside, I'm side swiped by the sweet, rotten stench of rubbish. The sole of my trainers splashes in a puddle. I feel water dampen the back of my trouser leg. On instinct, more than anything else, I reach down to my side, hover my fingertips over my holstered gun.

Ready to slip it out.

And *fire*.

I have to mentally tell myself that Tabby's on my side—that she's on *our* side.

That I need to just accept that and move on.

I hear the hairdryer engine of the hatchback rise up to a high-pitched hum; hit a reverse gear and plough backwards out of the side alley; leaving me behind.

I wonder if AA's going to pick me up afterwards.

If I actually come out the other side of this alive.

As the victor.

"Evening," Tabby says, giving me a smirk.

When I glance over her shadow-struck figure, I notice the gun she has down at her side. All holstered and ready. I wonder if the others—if Amy, AA and Tabby—have come up with some contingency plan; just in case I bottle it at the last moment.

Or maybe this is just a long con, and they're looking to have Tabby finish me off just as soon as I've finished with Brian.

I do my best to flush those paranoid thoughts from my brain, and have at least *some* success.

Beyond Tabby, I can see that the service door stands open, that she has left it propped open with some bulky—and no doubt *heavy*—cardboard box.

The interior is just as dark as it is outside.

As if the night has succeeded in purging the building.

In purging Mathewson Media.

Tabby reaches out; grips tight to my forearm.

She forces my eyes onto hers.

"Are you ready, Anna?"

I wonder if this might be my last chance to pull out, my last chance to say that I *can't* really do this at all . . . that I *won't* be able to flip my Kill Switch again.

But, deep down, I know that I can.

And, what's more, that it will be simple—*frighteningly easy, even* . . . once I get started.

I give Tabby a nod in reply.

"Good," she says, "then let's get on with it."

The two of us disappear into the darkened, night-time interior of Mathewson Media.

Chapter Forty-Three

THE AIR SMELLS strongly of disinfectant and floor polish.

I guess that Brian makes sure that even the service quarters of Mathewson Media are maintained spotless. He has always been something of a neat freak . . . somebody who doesn't like to have to face up to *filthy* messes . . . because if anybody's going to leave a filthy mess behind, it won't be Brian Mathewson.

Tabby seems to know where she's going, and she moves swiftly—*silently*—through anonymous corridors with that threadbare, office-block carpeting; and then up and down staircases. Through several metal doors.

These are the back corridors of power.

Perhaps even the embarrassed underside of the nation.

Where the kings are made; and then brought to their knees.

Up until tonight, at least.

Tabby leads the way through a door, and then into a larger room.

Only when I've taken several steps do I note the slick marble floor underfoot. The enormous, glass wall to my side. A little light from the streetlights outside manages to trickle in . . . but it creates nothing more than an impression of silhouettes; blurred angles.

I turn my attention to the chunky reception desk that must've seemed like the Gates of Heaven to many a politician; many a small-time celebrity hoping to make it large.

I look to all of the turnstiles, all of the demonic, red electronic eyes—standing static—waiting for fingerprints to be pressed down onto their tiny glass windows.

I glance to Tabby, but she only carries along, on her way.

I wonder, a touch dizzily, if we're going to leap over the top of the turnstiles, just like those people who refuse to pay for the Tube. As if we're just a pair of common young delinquents. As if we're not professionally trained killers after all.

But, no.

Tabby has a better idea.

I stand back as she approaches the turnstile, and then, glancing back over her shoulder, she gestures me close. To follow on her heels. With me standing so close to her that I can feel my breath bouncing back off her shoulders; so that I can breathe in her honey-like scent; Tabby presses her finger down hard on the scanner.

There's a smart *bleep* from somewhere within the mechanism.

I stay tight behind Tabby, and walk through the turnstile with her.

I have about enough time to glance up to the broad staircase bearing down on us when I hear the bullet whizz past my ear.

And pummel into the marble floor.

Chapter Forty-Four

I THINK to hold out my hands before I strike the ground.

My palms sting as they take the full force of the impact.

I roll over onto my side.

Another bullet flies through the air.

It strikes the floor just to the side of my ear.

Sharp pieces of marble fly up.

Scrape down the side of my face.

My heart pounds hard against my ribs.

A stale taste fills my mouth.

I glance about, searching for Tabby, but unable to see her.

Then I feel somebody grab me from behind.

Grab a fistful of my shirt.

Tabby.

And I rock backwards—just in time.

Another bullet spits out of the black.

Hammers into a pillar just above me.

My blood runs cold once more.

I resist the urge to look, to try and fathom where the shot came from.

Tabby keeps up her firm hold of my shirt—stops from moving a muscle.

The whole entrance hall of Mathewson Media goes deadly quiet. I strain my hearing, trying to catch the footsteps that're surely sounding. As our would-be killer stalks through the shadows, searching for the perfect vantage point.

So that they might finish with me and Tabby.

So that they might protect Brian.

Before I have a chance to get my thoughts together, Tabby grabs the back of my shirt all the tighter. Then she leans in and whispers in my ear, "Come *on!*" and drags me up to my feet, behind the cover of the pillar the most-recent bullet struck.

The two of us stand behind the pillar and I just about have the presence of mind to draw my gun. I slip it out of the holster, snap the safety off, and then look to Tabby—trying to garner some clue about what we're meant to do next.

Despite the killer stalking the shadows, I can't help asking, in the quietest voice I can muster, "Who is it?"

Tabby busies herself with her own handgun, checking the magazine to be sure that she's all set. And then she glances to me briefly, before turning her attention back to the hall behind us . . . on the other side of the pillar. "Deborah," she says, as if that explains everything.

Over to our left, I'm certain that I hear the *clack* of a high-heeled foot.

My breath hitches in my throat. "*Who?*" I say.

Still focussing on the gloom surrounding us—and on this Deborah character—Tabby mumbles under her breath, "Jesus, Brian's really got you in the dark, hasn't he . . ."

"Yes," I say, still looking into the darkness myself—determined that, between the two of us, we'll take Deborah down. "I thought that much was apparent."

Tabby raises her arm, stares along the sight of her gun and then shoots.

Out in the darkness, there's a scrabbling sound, and I get the impression that Tabby almost managed to find her target.

Perhaps next time.

"Brian's right-hand man," Tabby says, still facing into the darkness. "Or *woman*, I should say."

And there I was—once more—with delusions of grandeur; believing that Brian thought me special . . . as if *I* merited some form of preferential treatment. In the grand scheme of things, though, as it so often turns out, I'm nothing much more than a cog in the system; and now a part to be disposed of.

Another bullet rings out over our heads.

This time it shatters glass.

Sends it tinkling down to the ground, shattering as it lands.

My heart sticks in my throat.

There's something about the sound of breaking glass—a sort of fingernails-down-a-chalkboard sensation—that's never sat right with me.

Without another word on Deborah, Tabby grabs hold of my arm and tugs me along, out from behind the pillar and across the well-waxed marble floor.

More bullets come.

They cut into the wall behind us, almost as if the wall itself was exploding, sending those marble fragments bouncing about the place—scattering them at our feet.

Finally, we reach a set of stairs, another point where we can find some cover.

Crouching, pulling me down to the same level as her, Tabby speaks quickly—with a great sense of hurry. "Okay," she says, "this is the point where we split up—all right?"

I feel a flash of panic pass through me, and I remind myself that I'm a Big Girl now and I have Important Things To Do.

And that Tabby will be more than capable of handling this Deborah character.

Tabby points off into the darkness. "You need to get over to that back corridor—rush through it and up the three flights of steps." She pauses, glances back over my shoulder, then turns back to me, apparently finding nothing. "That'll bring you to another staircase. From there you just keep on going till you get up to the thirteenth floor; till you get to Brian's office." She pauses another moment, but this time she doesn't check our surroundings.

But she does give me a steely glare.

"You *have* been in Brian's office, haven't you?"

I stifle a smile, and give her a firm nod in response.

"Good," Tabby says, "then *go!*"

Although we don't exactly work out the intricacies of the plan, I know enough about working in a team that the idea is for Tabby to provide me with cover. That she's going to keep her eyes peeled for Deborah.

And I have hardly made it four paces in the direction Tabby indicated before I hear the bullets spurting out of the darkness once more. I implore myself to keep on going, knowing that so much as a second's hesitation would be more than enough for me to turn into an Anna-Harris shaped splodge of grease on the marble floor.

Tabby sends back shots.

I can't help but glance off in their direction.

208

To where Tabby shoots.

From behind a marble pillar, across the entrance hall, I spot her.

Deborah.

I catch sight of her blond hair.

The beige coat, sweeping her ankles.

And, now, the gun clenched in her hand.

The woman who met with me and AA—before our nightmare aeroplane trip.

The woman who met with me in the airport . . . who handed me the memory stick: the Death Log.

The woman who arrived at Mark's door.

Took his son away.

And, now, the woman who's trying to kill me.

To save Brian.

I force myself to keep my head low as I sprint off.

Several times I feel the heat of bullets passing close to my skin —but I have no time to process what they might mean.

That one of these bullets might well have my name written on it.

Finally, I reach the darkened corridor.

No more bullets come towards me.

I picture Deborah, no doubt attempting to retreat.

To rush backward in a desperate attempt to protect her boss.

But Tabby keeps her pinned down to her spot.

Behind the pillar.

Out of harm's way.

And now it's my job—and my job only—to take on Brian Mathewson.

Chapter Forty-Five

JUST LIKE TABBY INSTRUCTED, I get myself up to the thirteenth floor, utilising the back corridors and the never-ending, winding staircases. As I emerge up on the floor, I'm struck by memories of all the previous times I've come up here.

Of the many times when Brian dangled the carrot for me: the blood money.

And now that bloody money has returned.

For revenge.

I look to all the pillars which surround the floor, and then to the deathly quiet reception area which occupies the space just in front of the large walnut doors to Brian's office. I reflect how I *always* believed the entrance to Brian's office—not to mention his office *itself*—to be very much the wrong side of obscene.

As I tread carefully, wary of anybody who might linger in the shadows; any more top-secret—at least to me—bodyguards he might have lurking about the place.

Did he really believe that one woman would be enough to stop us?

That he could place all his trust in one person?

Some part of me simply *cannot* believe that.

No matter how hard I try.

As I close in on the enormous doors to Brian's office, I can feel a tingle passing down my spine. My lungs strain for more air than the full force of my breathing can allow. I grip my gun tightly, down by my thigh, ready for the attack to come from any direction. I constantly glance back over my shoulder, expecting to see the flash of a gun barrel, and then to embrace the bottomless darkness as the bullet puts an end to it all.

But these corridors are deserted.

Nobody except me and Brian now.

We'll sort this out between ourselves.

When I stand before the door, stare long and hard at the brass handles there, scratched-up and dull from years of use, I have the dizzy idea of knocking before going in.

I *always* knocked on Brian's office door whenever I came to visit.

And—for some reason—even now it feels like it shouldn't be any different.

No reason for me to neglect my manners.

Except that I've come here to kill him.

I give my gun a final once-over then turn the door handle.

Chapter Forty-Six

THE AIR of Brian's office reeks of cigar smoke and whisky.
I suppose that I should've guessed.

That Brian's decided if this *is* to be his last night on Earth then he's going to make the very best of it.

All the lights are down.

London is all lit up beyond the glass—its dulled orange street-lamps lighting up the skyline. Bringing out all those landmarks which, most days, seem to just blur into the background of the smog and filth: the Shard, the Gherkin, London Bridge . . . the Houses of Parliament . . .

Brian sees it all.

I turn my attention to one of the armchairs; its back to me. I observe the cloud of smoke rising from behind it. Lingering in the air above. I know that Brian sits on the other side, and that he's sitting with his legs crossed, his eyes prowling about the city below—considering his empire.

Thinking about just how far he's come.

And how far he has to fall.

My mouth tastes dry now, the mint which AA handed me back in the car a distant memory. I spot the drinks cabinet, to one side of Brian's office, and I spy the crystal decanter filled with fresh spring water—changed every four hours, day or night, at Brian's request.

I don't imagine Brian has made use of the water tonight.

That he's had no intention whatsoever of diluting his whisky.

As I tread closer to the back of the armchair, I feel a draught blowing about the room. And creeping in about the collar of my shirt. I give a slight shudder. It feels as if I shuck off a little nervous energy. As if I needed some sort of a release. Otherwise I might just have exploded.

I take one last breath before the final step.

I arrive beside the armchair.

And find myself staring at Brian in profile.

Chapter Forty-Seven

AT FIRST, I believe that he's made of stone. His flesh seems to have the texture of cold dough: that grisly, grey, lifeless shape to it . . . with only a dull sheen implying life within.

On instinct, I cast my eyes over Brian's entire body, getting a quick impression that, because of the very stillness of Brian, the way that he sits there, in the armchair, dressed in a tuxedo, and staring out ahead; that he has decided to commit suicide rather than allow himself to be killed.

Or that—*somehow*—he has been replaced by a wax dummy.

Some eighteenth-century parlour trick employed in order to fool the most cursory of inspections.

But I see that's not what he's done here.

I take stock of Brian again.

And I see how he gently holds a glass of whisky; only a trickle of amber liquid in the base of the tumbler now. My eyes track the cigar as it smoulders away, pinched firmly between a pair of his fingers in the other hand. Its tip glows a dimming red as it puffs bluish-grey, coils of smoke.

Brian's eyes, as I imagine they always do at this hour, look sodden in their sockets. As if they're swilling about within their own personal fish tanks. Nobody ever tells him when he's had enough, and that's the way he likes it.

I suppose that insomnia demands a vice.

". . . Brian?" I say, holding my gun down at my side, and surprising myself at how flimsy—how *weak*—my voice sounds.

Brian remains facing forwards, continuing to cling tightly to his tumbler of whisky and his cigar.

Without a word to me, he finally moves.

He raises his cigar up to his lips, sucks on it for several seconds. Brings the cigar back down.

After what might be only a few seconds, or as much as a minute, he blows out the cigar smoke. It wafts up against the glass and then sweeps its way along it, covering the cityscape outside.

That done, he presses his glass of whisky up against his lips.

He sucks at the remaining liquid within with the hunger and appetite that a baby suckling at its mother's nipple might show.

He allows the emptied glass to sit on the armrest.

And then, very slowly, he turns to me.

Gives me a sly, knowing smile.

A smile that I prepare to extinguish.

For good.

Chapter Forty-Eight

EVEN as I bring the gun up to Brian Mathewson's temple I feel as if I'm on the back foot. I know that—*still*—the wily old dog has another trick up his sleeve. That he wouldn't have allowed me to get to this point; gone to all the trouble of displaying his weakness so obviously to me; if he didn't have some sort of plan for counter-attack.

Brian's smile widens, and his eyelids droop low, as if he's preparing for a long and well-deserved sleep. When he finally speaks to me, the tone of his voice is raspy, and his words slightly slurred. "It's been a good ride, hasn't it, Anna?"

I scrabble for something to say to that, but all I can muster is a vague *croak* from the back of my throat. Neither an affirmation or a negation.

Just a sound.

My hand quivers as I hold the gun there, and although I know that I have to do it—that between us, between me, and Tabby, Amy and AA we've decided that this has to happen for our survival, as well as the bettering of the nation—I find my mind blocked.

My finger just won't twitch on the trigger.

Brian continues to stare on out through the glass, as if I'm not there at all. As if he's only speaking to me on the phone. "I always wanted it to be you." His tone is crisp, cool . . . he seems to have shed the slightly drunken tremble which accompanied his previous words. "I always liked you best."

"If you *liked* me so much then why didn't you make me your personal bodyguard—why did you give it to that blond woman; to Deborah?"

Still staring out of the window, Brian gives a pout and a shrug. "That's just business; the way the cards are dealt. It would take a magician to change that."

"You *are* a magician," I reply. "Or at least the closest thing to one in the real world."

Brian gives a vague smile and a shake of his head. "Thank you, Anna, that's very kind of you to say so . . . but I think you're overstating the extent of my power, somewhat. I wouldn't want to blow my own whistle on that, so to speak."

I shake my head right back at him, still very aware that I hold a gun to his head. "No," I say. "You have your fingerprints on everything: celebrity, the media . . . *politics* . . . there's nothing that you couldn't influence without a quick phone call here; calling in a favour there." I breathe in deeply, feel the air quench my lungs for the first time since I set foot in Mathewson Media tonight. "What does it feel like?" I say. "To wield all that power?"

Brian sits very still for one or two seconds and then, seemingly out of nowhere, he chuckles. All his features soften in that moment. And the chuckles shake his body too.

"Is it funny?" I say. "Is the world reduced to being nothing more than an anthill, their little systems; their little *lives*; all ready to be stomped on at will?" I pause a moment and then correct myself. "At *your* will?"

Brian chuckles harder still. He doubles over himself, sets his hands on his knees. He shakes his head as if this is the funniest joke he's ever heard. He reaches up to wipe the tears from his eyes.

At first, I'm sure that this must be some sort of ruse—that he's going to grab for a weapon he's kept, until now, concealed beneath his chair.

But, when he comes up for air, he has nothing except his own bare hands.

He looks at me with those walnut eyes of his. The smile fades slowly from his lips, replaced by a more sobered expression. It's one of those unnerving moments, when the happy-go-lucky, drunken-fool exterior of Brian Mathewson seems to tumble down; as if it was nothing more than a poorly hung bedsheet on a clothes line.

And the reality—the *real thing*—stares out from underneath.

Concealed no more.

"Tell me, Anna," he says, his voice gruff—*sharp.* "What exactly is it that I have done to you; how is it that I have stoked your rage so much that I have brought you up here—to my office —so that you might murder me? Hmm?"

I try not to allow myself to think.

I grip the gun tighter still.

A bead of sweat rolls down the side of my face—tickling my skin as it goes.

Another shudder passes through me, and, as I see it off, a twitching I can't control passes through my nerves, and almost prompts me to squeeze the trigger.

But I hold myself firm.

Tell myself to keep it together.

To keep papering over the cracks.

Brian continues, turning in his armchair so that he stares right up at me, so that the barrel of the gun now points directly at his forehead, "Let's review the evidence, eh?" He pulls on one of his fingers. "One, I keep you employed doing what you and I know you do the best in this world."

He cocks his head to one side, flashes a grin at me.

I see his yellowed teeth; the years of cigar-smoking and whisky-drinking.

"Two," he says, pulling another finger, and with the grin disappearing, "I give you a way out, a means for you to feel secure, that memory stick with *all* that information on me and my operations."

He widens his eyes as if spooked.

But I can tell by his posture, by the confidence of his speech, that only one person is in control here.

And it's not me.

As if to confirm this, he adds, "The *Death Log*."

Although I fully expect him to smile at this—at showing that he has me monitored, that he's been *spying* on me . . . and that he's privy to even my most intimate of thoughts . . . he doesn't show any sign of self-satisfaction.

But, then again, I suppose that surveillance—*deception*—is all in a day's work for Brian Mathewson.

"Three," Brian continues, "I leave you alone . . . I do nothing to either hunt you down, or to '*resolve*' "—he actually makes the bunny ears with his fingers here—"the complications which your continued existence presents my operation."

I decide to allow the whole flying-me-out-to-a-Caribbean-island-and-trying-to-have-me-killed-by-local-militia thing out of this for the time being . . . not wanting to ruin his streak.

However, I *do* take him up on one aspect.

"You burned down my house," I say, feeling my gun again quiver in my hand.

One of the rules I've always tried to stick to is *avoiding* making the hit personal.

But it doesn't get much more personal than burning down someone's home . . .

"No, Anna," Brian says, as if I'm testing his patience, as if I'm *not* the one with the gun up against his forehead. "Charlie Branwick had your house burned down, and, as I'm sure you've figured out by now, his daughter, Amy Douglas, was the one who lit the match. So to speak."

I give him a sly smile. "You mean to tell me that you had *nothing* to do with it—that you didn't want to get revenge for what we did on the island?"

"What *did* you do on the island?" Brian says, arching an eyebrow.

The way he says it suggests he knows *exactly* what I did.

That he's feigning ignorance.

Or, at the very least, he's *willing* to feign ignorance over the whole affair.

My chest tightens and my blood pounds up to my temples.

I know that there's no time.

That this should've been as simple as me stealing into his office, firing the shot into his brain, and then walking away.

The mistake was to allow him to speak.

To allow him a chance to *defend* himself.

Maybe a life in justice for me isn't so far-fetched as it once seemed.

I decide now's the time for me to play the last card in my hand; the final thing that I can think of. "What about Nathan— my *boyfriend Mark's*—son?"

Brian stares back at me for a long while. And then he turns to look out of the window once more, to peruse the London skyline. The way that he sits there, in the armchair, his shoulders hardly rising and falling as he breathes, and how he displays total calm on the exterior, makes me begin to believe that he's not human at all.

That he doesn't have blood flowing in his veins like the rest of us.

That he can never be killed.

"You backed me into a corner." Brian says. "Nothing more— nothing less." He turns back to me, meets my eye. "I needed a bargaining position and so I took it."

I almost laugh at his choice of words. "A *bargaining* position?"

"Yes," Brian says, and then he gives a shake of his head, and flaps his hands up into the air, to indicate the office, and—I imply —Mathewson Media in general. "I'm not exactly *hiding* am I, Anna? I mean, if I *really* wanted to go to ground, if I wanted to avoid your little *troupe* then there're places I would go." He shakes his head again. "No, I stayed right here—exactly where you knew to find me."

"Yeah?" I say. "Then what's with that blond bombshell assassin you have stalking about the entrance hall?"

Brian shrugs. "I needed to ensure that you would come alone —that I would be able to speak with someone who would see sense."

"You don't think that AA, or Amy, or Tabby would see sense?"

Just in saying their names, I feel as if I've betrayed them.

But I couldn't help it.

Once Brian's got me talking, it's extremely difficult to stop.

Almost as if I came here—to Brian's office—looking for a reason *not* to end him.

I turn my attention back to Nathan. "You didn't want a bargaining position—you wanted *blackmail*."

"Excuse me for being so impertinent," Brian says, going cross-eyed as he stares into the barrel of my gun, "but couldn't what you're doing right now be interpreted as blackmail?"

I suppose he's got me there.

Chapter Forty-Nine

"A RE YOU REALLY that bloodthirsty, Anna?" Brian says, continuing to stare into the barrel of my gun. "Do you desire to notch up another kill so badly?"

I keep the gun still—*fixed* on Brian's forehead.

And, of course, I offer no answer.

"Don't you crave another sort of life? A way for you to simply *walk away* from all of this?"

"Where's the boy?" I say, trying to distract myself, to turn the focus of the conversation onto Nathan: Mark's adopted son.

Brian holds his palms up flat, as if to absolve himself of responsibility. "He's in the *system* now, Anna—nothing for me to do about it." He draws in a breath, and puffs himself up to what seems like twice his height. "I did nothing illegal, at all. I think if you ask *Mark* he'll only confirm that the paperwork he has is not up to scratch. If anybody has done anything illegal then it's Mark himself."

"Who *cares* about paperwork?" I say. "He was Mark's *family*."

"I'll tell you who cares about paperwork, Anna—*everyone*. Without it the whole world would be a mess; people would have to start taking one another at their word. There would be a total absence of any sort of *proof*. It's one thing to *attest* to something being true, but it's quite another to possess the *evidence*."

Brian gives the final syllable of 'evidence' an almost snakelike *hiss*.

I press my tongue up against the back of my teeth, and keep pushing as hard as I can until I feel pain flashing through my gums. "If I . . ." I begin, then think better of it . . . and then —*finally*—decide that I should at least float the prospect. "Will you be able to get Mark back his son if I let you go?"

Brian widens his eyes and gives what—under any other set of circumstances—might be a pleasant smile. "I could certainly take it into consideration—I could grease a few palms; call in a few *favours*, as you put it." He cocks his head to one side. "There're things about this country that would *sicken* you if you only knew the truth—if you only knew how to use that *Death Log* in an appropriate manner . . . to properly exercise your power."

It's then that my mind snags onto what this is really all about.

And it's almost like an alarm bell ringing inside my skull.

Its sound bouncing back and forth.

Deafening.

Even then, though, as the thought tumbles through my mind, I can't quite find a way to believe it. To *truly* believe it. And yet it all tumbles out through my lips. "You wanted this," I say. "You *planned* all of this." I blink several times, feeling the gloom of the office beginning to creep up on me from all sides. "This is your endgame—you *want* me to go to the media with the contents of the Death Log . . . you want them to know all about your sordid operations, all about those involved."

Brian meets my eye for a long while.

He's not smiling now.

When he speaks, his voice is finely cut.

Crystal clear.

"Yes, Anna." he says. "That's precisely it. Clever girl."

I can almost hear the sarcasm *dripping* off his words.

Splattering into puddles at his feet.

"I know I'm not going to live forever," he says. "*Nobody* lives forever—"

But I have a fiery sensation at the pit of my gut and I know that I have to keep on speaking; keep on unravelling these tangled webs which Brian has woven, not only about me and AA —*Tabby too*—but around the entire world. "You *want* me to kill you now—and for me to go and release the information on the Death Log. So that the whole world knows." Then I feel a pinching sensation in my stomach, as if someone has just jabbed me with a needle. "You want the world to burn."

A profound silence fills the office.

My heart beats so hard that I'm *certain* it must echo about the room.

That it must be giving the whole of Mathewson Media a percussive soundtrack.

When I believe myself to be edging away—out of consciousness—Brian finally speaks. "You have no idea, Anna, the sorts of things I've seen in my life. The *filthiness* of the world. Inside and out, something needs to change. And the only way to do that is through the media. The whole world *must* know the truth. And— *what's more*—they must have the evidence. The names, the places, and, most important of all, how much it all cost."

I feel a dizziness strike me.

Suddenly, the whole world begins to spin.

I wonder if someone *has* injected me with something.

If the blond woman—*somehow*—has snuck up behind me and stuck me with a needle.

But I bring the scene before me: Brian Mathewson sat in his armchair; back into focus.

He continues to stare up into my eyes.

Locking me in his gaze.

I turn to face him. "This wasn't a bargain at all," I say. "You just took Nathan's son so that I would *think* there was the prospect of a bargain to be had."

A smile tweaks the corner of Brian's mouth. "If you don't kill me, Anna, then the second you step out of that door, I'll throw myself out of the window. They'll have to scrape me up off the tarmac tomorrow morning."

A giddiness passes through my brain.

Suddenly it's a struggle to stay on my feet.

For the first time in our conversation, I allow the gun to droop down to my thigh.

But I keep a strong grip on it . . . knowing that I need to keep my senses sharp; that I have to be prepared for *anything*.

I look back to Brian, stare into his eyes. "But I won't release the Death Log," I say. "I'll keep it a secret—I'll *destroy* it."

Brian's smile widens. "Do you really think that I was pinning *all* my hopes on you, Anna? Do you really believe that I would've attempted to pull off such a *majestic* masterstroke without having a solid backup?"

My instinct is to answer no, but I also feel that this could quite easily be a bluff.

"You must understand that this shall be my masterpiece," Brian says. "That everything which has led up to this point, all of the clients I've served, all the money I've made"—he pounds his fist on the arm of his chair—"this *building* I own as a result of that success; it's all a bagatelle compared to what's coming. Compared to the mess that I'll leave behind as my legacy."

For some reason, perhaps just the pure ridiculousness of the thing, a smile sneaks onto my lips and I find myself replying, "Kind of like history's biggest ever whistle-blower?"

"Yes," he says, smiling back at me. "Something like that."

My brain comes clear again, and I regain some control over my trembling.

I bring my gun up—level it at Brian's head, and prepare to pull the trigger. "Do you want to know what my masterpiece will be?" I say.

"What?" Brian says, still grinning.

"Killing you."

And then I pull the trigger.

Chapter Fifty

MY FEET seem to have a mind of their own.

In fact, my entire body functions on autopilot.

The second that I observe Brian Mathewson's lifeless body flop out of the armchair and *thump* down on the floor of his office, I know that the illusion is broken.

That I've either fallen into a big trap.

Or I've safely avoided a landmine.

I leave his office behind, slipping my gun back into its holster.

Once I'm out through the doors, I bring them shut behind me, as if I was attempting to make it seem that Brian's been locked in his office all night.

That—*somehow*—a bullet has found its way into his brain.

As I walk away from my boss's office, and back down the staircase, towards the entrance hall, I wonder if killing has some sort of a therapeutic pull for me.

If what Brian said was right.

That this really *is* what I'm best at.

As I slip through the darkened corridors, and back to the entrance hall, I half expect to hear bullets: to witness Tabby and Deborah still trading gunfire.

But it's disturbingly quiet.

I stand still on the spot, look around. My heart throbs in my eardrums. I have no fear now—no fear surrounding my demise coming to pass right here, on this spot. And, in a strange way, it gives me a certain strength.

Finally, when it feels like I've been standing in the gloom of the entrance hall for *hours*, I hear a familiar voice from out of the darkness.

It's Tabby.

"Is it done?" she says.

I hold my breath, feeling as if it hasn't happened—hasn't *really* happened—until I actually put it into words.

So I do. "Brian Mathewson's dead," I say.

Tabby presses her lips tightly together, and gives me a stern nod. Then she glances back over her shoulder.

I follow her gaze.

See the prostrate body lying there.

On the marble floor.

The blond assistant of Brian's—Deborah . . . well and truly deceased.

"Come on," Tabby says, gripping hold of my sleeve. "AA will be waiting for us."

Only as Tabby grips tight to me, does something deep buried in my brain protest—tell me that there's still some unfinished business here. Finally, I manage to find my voice. "Nathan," I say. "Mark's *son.*"

Tabby glances back at me, obviously feeling the resistance of my standing still—like some sort of a stubborn boulder, refusing to be budged. "Who?" she says.

"Brian," I say, feeling a touch giddy now, "he said that he would be able to bring Mark . . . *my boyfriend's* . . . son back to him."

Tabby shakes her head. "Anna," she says, "I've got no idea what you're talking about, but we need to get moving. It's not safe for us to linger here. We have no idea what Brian might have in store—what sort of unpleasantness he has planned post-mortem."

I manage a slight smile, but don't resist Tabby tugging me on further still.

There's a *huge* amount that I still need to fill her and AA in on.

Chapter Fifty-One

SILENCE is the prevailing detail of the car journey.

AA trundles us along, in the estate car from earlier.

We've rounded the corner, got ourselves a good five minutes' drive away from Mathewson Media before AA even *dares* to raise his voice. To ask a question.

"Brian's really dead?" he says, hands clamping the wheel, eyes dead-set on the road ahead.

Sitting in the passenger seat, and feeling as if this is becoming the perennial question, I give him a nod in reply.

He slips me a sidelong glance and then gives me a nod back.

He shows no sign of being pleased to hear this information.

No sign of being disappointed, *either.*

Despite feeling as if I'm presenting a cool exterior, I can't help the constant *tap-tap* of my heart up in my throat. As if my body is still processing whatever trauma has been stoked by my killing Brian Mathewson.

"So," Tabby says, from the back seat, "what now?"

The question just hangs in the air for the longest time.

AA continues to steer the car forwards, his brain apparently elsewhere. Then, as if something has been triggered in his mind, he blurts out, "Look, Anna, I remember all that stuff you said about being honest, and, well, I've been doing a lot of thinking about it . . . the truth of the thing is that it's been difficult—*really* difficult . . ."

Before AA can even blunder his way through whatever moral ground he's *attempting* to define, I cut him off. "Whatever it is," I say, "it doesn't matter anymore, okay?"

AA stays quiet for several moments, glances back over his shoulder, to Tabby in the back seat and then he continues, "No, Anna," he says, "trust me, this is important, this will change things. This will change *everything*—I'm sure."

I feel a flash of frustration about AA keeping up with all this mystery, refusing to accept my forgiveness . . . for him and Amy; and Tabby, skulking about in the shadows while my house burned down and my life—not to mention the lives of those I *love*—were in constant danger.

"Listen," I say, "can't we just draw a line under this whole thing? Allow it all to be forgotten? We don't even need to so much as *see* one another again if we don't feel like it."

Another long silence grips the interior of the car.

Finally Tabby leans forwards, rests her elbows on the backrests of the front seats. "What AA's trying to say, Anna," she says, "is that what we did here—*all this*—has been for Brian . . . it was what he *wanted* us to do."

My chest tightens.

My blood runs cold.

Suddenly, every muscle in my body draws tight.

As if responding to this revelation, AA guns the engine, driving the car along faster.

When I reach for the door handle to my side of the car, contemplating jumping *despite* the new rush of speed, it has no effect. AA has engaged the child lock on it.

I swivel about in my seat, suddenly feeling as if I've been asleep all along, and that I've only awoken just now to find that there're thousands of spiders crawling all over my bed.

Realising that the door handle's not going to be any good, I turn my attention to AA . . . and it's then that—out of the corner of my eye—I notice the barrel of the gun pointed at me, from out of the back seat, from out of Tabby's hand.

"Anna," Tabby says, her voice flat, and calm, and *clearly* trying to make me understand in that way arch villains seem only able to pull off. "You've got to trust us—all right?" She draws a deep breath. "If you listen to what we have to say, don't make a fuss about it, then I think there'll be a way for us to get Nathan back."

As I feel Tabby's gun on me, and think about how she pretended not to even have *heard* Nathan's name earlier on, I turn back to the front.

Turn my attention to the road ahead.

And to those painted-on white lines sweeping under the car at a rapid pace.

Chapter Fifty-Two

O NCE IT'S BEEN ESTABLISHED—without anything so fancy as *ambiguity*—that there's *zero* chance of me opening the passenger door and escaping the car, AA slows down to a more palatable speed.

The silence falls on my shoulders like a dead weight.

Almost as if I stand in the sea, just about out of my depth, invisible bags of sand on my shoulders, slowly—*but surely*— weighing me down.

Slowly drowning me.

When I can't take it any longer, I turn to AA and say, "Now will you tell me where we're going?"

AA keeps his eyes on the road ahead, then mumbles, almost too quietly to be heard, ". . . To Amy."

A thrill passes through my blood.

I glance into the back seat, see that Tabby has laid her gun down on her lap now . . . something of an improvement from having it aimed at the back of my head, at least.

I turn back to AA. "Mark's house?" I say.

AA nods in reply.

I feel as if my lungs swell with air.

When I can no longer take the pressure pushing my ribcage outwards, I let loose a long, unbroken exhale.

AA pulls us up on the curb outside the house.

I guess the time to be a little after midnight now.

All the houses on the street have their lights switched off— some with only their porchlights still switched on. Another few more of them have tea lights in their gardens. Other than that, the only light on the road comes from the orange wash of the streetlamps.

AA turns in his seat, nods to Tabby.

He keeps the engine running as Tabby slips out of the back seat, bringing in a gentle gust of freezing-cold air, before slamming the door shut behind her. She arrives at my door, at the window, the gun still very much down at her thigh, and ready to be brought up at any second.

Tabby pauses there, and I wonder what the delay is.

"Anna?" AA says, and then nods down to my own thigh.

To the holstered gun I have there.

I reach down for it, unbutton the holster.

I think—for a *quick* moment—about turning it first onto AA, and then onto Tabby, but somehow the logical part of my brain kicks in; tells me that if I committed such a rash action, managed to get myself killed in a shootout on the curb just beyond Mark's driveway, then there'll be little-to-*no* chance of him getting Nathan back.

Not much of an argument for being able to provide a safe environment for a child when there're shootouts happening almost on your front lawn.

With a bitter taste in my mouth, I hand my gun over to AA.

Then—and *only* then—Tabby unlatches my door from the outside.

And I get out.

Ready for whatever's coming next.

Chapter Fifty-Three

I T'S SOMEWHAT surreal to find myself standing between AA and Tabby on Mark's front doorstep, all of us waiting for the response to the ring of the bell.

From within, I hear the sound of stirring, a cough, and then the door opens.

Mark stands there, on the doorstep.

He has on a washed-out, blue-white dressing gown. Over the top of a pair of green, red-and-gold patterned pyjama bottoms. On his feet, he wears a pair of novelty bunny rabbit slippers. His long, hair hangs down to his shoulders, and I can tell that—although he's dressed for it—he certainly wasn't in bed.

In fact, when his eyes slip across mine; and he takes a step back into the front hall of his house, I catch a whiff of that familiar scent of sawdust . . . perhaps he's been taking his real world frustrations out on his craft:

Getting some work done.

Although I have an explanation all ready to offer Mark, he

looks away from me, his eyes turning to the floor, as if it won't be necessary.

I tread in over the threshold, still feeling uneasy to have AA and Tabby keeping their collective watchful gaze fixed on me. I hear the door slam shut on my heels.

The impact sends a rumbling vibration up through the soles of my trainers. The warmth of the house flushes right up to my cheeks, and kindles a heating feeling down in the pit of my stomach.

Without a word of greeting to Mark, AA says, "Where is she?"

"The living room," Mark replies.

I glance to AA, then look to Tabby, before finally bringing my gaze back to Mark.

"You first," AA says to Mark.

With a quick glance over us, Mark treads into the sitting room.

There's a twisting sensation in my stomach, and I can't help feeling that Brian Mathewson's ghost is very much present here. That wherever he might be now—in whatever spiritual form—he's bringing himself to bear on this situation.

If what he told me in his office is to be believed then this is just what he wanted.

I enter the sitting room after Mark.

The main light in the room is switched off; only lamps beat back the darkness, their warming, yellow glow shining up the walls.

The well-loved, turtle-green sofa stretches out before the TV.

The TV itself is switched on but the sound is turned to Mute.

It's on a twenty-four-hour news channel, and—*I can't help wondering*—that it's exclusive purpose for being switched on is to

witness the confirmation of the demise of Brian Mathewson . . .
a somewhat morbid reason if ever there was one, though I'm not
exactly one to talk . . .

Amy perches on the edge of the sofa, her knees pinched
together, wearing a light-pink summer dress over the top of a pair
of jeans. When she turns to face me, she gives me the frailest of
smiles. "Hi, Anna," she says, and then nods to AA and Tabby. "Is
it really true? Did you really do it?"

My mind flashes back to the car ride here, and how—
shortly after my status had shifted from Hero's Welcome to
Unwilling Passenger—AA placed a hurried, monosyllabic
phone call.

One of those calls which can only possibly function if both
parties know exactly the reason for it taking place. Those staccato
yes's and no's could only have meaning in the context of the
demise of Brian Mathewson.

I take a step into the sitting room, feeling Mark's eyes on the
side of my face. But I say nothing for the time being. When I
eventually *do* attempt to clear things up, it's going to be an awfully
messy conversation.

I look to Amy, and finally answer her question with a nod.

Just as when I informed AA of our employer's demise, I
didn't exactly expect a wide-eyed smile, or for there to be
balloons, streamers and party horns going off from all directions;
I didn't expect much more than a stoic nod.

Which is what Amy gives me now.

As if this was what she expected.

As if this was just part of the *Plan.*

I glance back over my shoulder, to Tabby and AA, doing my
best to forget—for the moment—that Mark's not here at all.
"You're the backup, aren't you?" I say. "The backup that Brian

told me about—if I didn't have the guts to publish the Death Log?"

"No, Anna," Amy says, replying from the sofa. "*I'm* the backup."

I turn back to her.

I study her childlike, straight blond hair.

She has her attention back on the TV screen, on the constantly moving crimson ribbon at the bottom. White text on top:

BREAKING NEWS — MEDIA MOGUL BRIAN MATH-EWSON FOUND DEAD

Chapter Fifty-Four

THE WHOLE ROOM steeps in silence.

In the end, it's Mark who speaks first. His voice is low, factual, almost as if he's been drugged with something—and, I tell myself right then, that if I find out Amy has gone to the extent of *drugging* Mark then it'll be the very last thing she does.

"That name," Mark says. "Sounds familiar."

My throat tightens.

I know that I owe Mark *several* explanations.

So at least this is somewhere to start.

"Yes," I say, my voice croaking and my throat feeling almost impossibly dry. "We saw him, a few days ago, on TV."

I look to Mark, watch as he gives a nod, as his mouth latches open in understanding.

And then, for the briefest of moments, his beautiful hazel eyes catch mine.

No anger. Not yet. Just confusion.

I turn back to Amy. "Where is it?" I say. "The Death Log?"

Amy aims her steely glare at the TV screen, just as a picture of Brian Mathewson pops up. Just as I always picture him in my mind, he holds a tumbler of whisky; a smouldering cigar smokes away in his other hand. And he wears a wide—*wide*—smile. All of the faces surrounding him are blurred out for privacy's sake . . .no doubt, to protect the anonymous, very high—very *powerful*—individuals who have a high stake in Brian Mathewson's death.

But, then again, who in the political spheres doesn't?

Or *didn't?*

Amy looks back to me. Her eyes widen a touch. She swallows then looks to AA and to Tabby, the two of them still standing off to one side, as if they're just the muscle here, as if they're only present so that I don't *blow up*, or whatever it is they imagine I'll do.

"It's safe," Amy replies, then turns back to the screen. "I'll keep it safe."

A squirming sensation takes hold of my stomach.

I pivot, aim my glare at AA and Tabby. "You're going to do just what he said, aren't you?" I say. "You're going to allow him to get his dying wish."

This time it's AA who speaks up.

His expression remains neutral, lips slightly pert. "No, Anna," he says, "We're just going to keep our hands on it until we can make a rational decision."

I look to Mark—as if he might have some sort of clue about what's going on here—and then back to Amy. "Please," I say, "Brian Mathewson's gone—he's *dead*. I killed him myself. How can you possibly feel obliged to do anything for him?" I give another exasperated shake of the head and then look back to Tabby and AA . . . my voice coming too close to a begging tone for my liking.

"Just destroy it—he hasn't got any *power* any longer."

But my comments are only received by yet more stony silence.

And it's in that moment where I feel, quite depressingly, that I'm the only sane person in the room.

Chapter Fifty-Five

W E STAND AROUND in the sitting room for longer than I can possibly imagine. Everybody in the room stands in silence, watching the TV screen; Mark included, even though he can't possibly comprehend the significance of the situation.

The whole time, with us just standing there, nobody thinks to unmute the TV.

In the end, it falls to me to turn it off.

When I do, it's as if a spell is broken. As I stand before them, I feel a furry, warm body rub up against my leg and—*sure enough*—when I look down I see that it's Lizzie there. I reach down, scoop her up in my arms and then hold her to my chest, feeling her purring away in response.

Realising that nobody else is going to speak—nobody is going to break through Lizzie's constant *purrs*—I look about the room and say, "What happens now?"

Everyone in the room—Mark aside—attempts to avoid my

gaze, as if by just not meeting my eye it'll make the question go away. I think long and hard about my next comment, if it might —or might *not*—be the straw which breaks the proverbial camel's back.

"Can you help us to get Nathan back?" I say, to AA and Tabby.

Although I can feel Mark's searing glare up against the side of my face, almost bringing me out in a blush, I do my best to ignore it.

Tabby looks to AA, and then AA looks back at her.

In the end, AA gives Tabby a nod and she slips out of the room.

Along with that gun she was subtly keeping down at her side.

She was so subtle about it that I doubt Mark even noticed she had it at all.

Tabby brings the door to the sitting room shut behind her.

I look back over to Amy, and then to AA. "Is this the end, then?" I say.

No response from either AA or Amy.

"Look," I say, growing impatient now, "why don't you just tell me *everything*, huh? I can tell that you all did this for Brian, that this was *all* set up for Brian."

Unexpectedly, Mark pipes up. "But I thought Brian was the one who snuffed it."

All three of us—me, AA and Amy—all turn to stare at Mark, as if he hasn't been able to cotton onto what's happened from what he's overheard so far.

Mark just stands where he is, and then gives a shrug of his shoulders. "Anybody want a cup of tea?"

There's a vague murmur between the three of us, and Mark

takes this opportunity to scarper from the room; to head off into the kitchen.

Leaving me, Amy and AA all alone.

I turn to Amy again, then say, "Don't you realise that if you publish the Death Log then it'll bring the country to its knees? That there's information on that memory stick which could potentially bring about a revolution?"

Another silence.

But I don't allow it to affect me.

"Is this *really* what you want?" I say, and then shake my head. "Forget Brian for a second, okay? Forget that he has anything at all to do with this. I want both of you"—I glance back at AA—"to think this through thoroughly, and to decide for yourselves if you *really* want to bring the entire system down."

A longer silence.

Out in the hallway, beyond the sitting room door, I can hear Tabby issuing orders on her phone. I know that at any moment she will re-enter the room. My only hope of convincing AA and Amy to see some sense is if she's *outside* the room . . . then—just maybe—I can make all three of them see sense . . . see that they're not trapped anymore.

Not trapped by Brian Mathewson.

Before I can start up again, Amy stirs from her seat on the sofa, and says, "My father died for this."

I remark at how emotionless; how matter-of-fact she manages to keep the tone of her voice. I speculate that, had I been in the same situation as her, then I wouldn't have been able to act so calm . . . or maybe I would; who knows just how these things will affect a cold-blooded killer?

Amy continues, "It feels that if we don't go through with the plan, if we don't do what Brian's asked of us, that it will all have been a waste." She glances up at me. "The things Brian's told me about—the *corruption*—how honest, hard-working people are left behind in the mores and the excesses of the political class . . ." she shakes her head ". . . I've never been political, nothing like that, but what Brian was doing—what he *wants* to do in releasing the Death Log—well, it seems for the Greater Good."

That final phrase strikes me strangely.

It draws a dry laugh up from the pit of my throat.

And, what's more, I only realise I've laughed at all when I notice Amy and AA both staring at me; as if I've totally lost my mind.

Then again, perhaps I have.

"Amy," I say, "you can count on it that the 'Greater Good' would've been the very last thought on Brian's mind . . . what he wants . . . what he *wanted* was to be remembered. The fact that he'll bring the country down is *immaterial*—he only wants his legacy to be that *he* was the one to bring about the revolution."

AA speaks up, out of nowhere.

To tell the truth, I almost forgot that he was there in the room with us at all.

"And there *I* was," AA says, "thinking that Brian would be content with having snuffed out lives at will; with having every celebrity, nationwide, at his beck and call; at having held half the country's politicians on a chain." He glances up, meets my eye for a moment. "But it wasn't enough for him, was it? It wasn't enough to secure the *proper* legacy he always wished for."

I can't help but smile back at AA, thankful that I've at least got through to *one* of them. And, when I look back to Amy, I see that she's shaking her head, eyes fixed on the carpet, off in her own world of grief and confusion.

I decide the time is right for the Woman's Touch.

I go over to Amy and, very carefully, take a seat beside her. Then, even more carefully still, I lay a hand on her shoulder. Feel the velvet-smooth exposed flesh. "Listen," I say, "your father didn't die in vain . . . you have to understand that. What Brian told you, it was all for *him*; it was all his own selfish desires. Now, though, we have a choice. We can be the adults here."

I draw another breath, glance back at AA.

Then turn to Amy once again.

"Instead of getting caught up in these games, in *publishing* the contents of the Death Log, we can turn our backs on it, tell one another that—*really*—this is the way the game has always been played; power *corrupts* . . . and that's *all* it ever does. The only thing which keeps the truth from getting out, as Brian would've said, is Good Press."

Amy remains still for a long while, and then, slowly, she turns her face to mine. She gives a slight smile. "Even if we did bring it all down, the same would just happen again, wouldn't it?"

"Well," I say, smiling back at her, and then shooting AA a knowing glance, "maybe it'd take a while longer now that Brian Mathewson's not around to grease the wheels."

Six Months Later

I FEEL my heart humming up in my throat.

I've never liked *blades* . . . something about them sends my bones to jelly, causes all my muscles to seize up.

Some assassin *I* am.

I stare down at the pair of secateurs in my gloved hand, and then to the rose bush—in desperate need of pruning. When I breathe in, I catch the gentle fragrances of Mark's back garden: all the tulips; the lavender; and the lush, thick carpet of grass.

The early-evening sun shines down on the backs of my shoulders—the flesh exposed just above my strappy top; and it feels great to be getting a little colour back into my skin.

It feels almost as if I've gone as white as a snowflake this past winter.

In the distance, I can hear a lawnmower starting up, and a faint whiff of petrol to go with it. As I move in for the coup de grâce on the current rose bud, I catch another taste of the delicious smoked salmon which Mark 'threw together' a little earlier for Sunday lunch.

"Anna?"

I turn my head, look to the back porch.

And I see Nathan standing there.

I smile back at him, and he smiles at me.

"Tea?" he says.

I rise up off my haunches, reach down and brush off a few rose petals that cling to the front of my jeans. "That'd be great, thanks!" I call back to him.

He gives me a mock salute in reply and disappears back inside the house.

As I settle back down before the rose bush, secateurs gripped tightly in my hand, I can hear the rhythmic sawing coming from Mark's workshop. Just like always, he said that he would only be 'ten minutes' to 'just finish up' but he's actually been in there for the best part of two hours now.

Not that it bothers me.

I've got my own stuff to do.

I bring about the premature end of another dozen or so rose buds before I hear a familiar—if slightly muffled—*miaow* at my heels.

I turn to look and see that it's Lizzie, and then—somewhat unexpectedly—that she has an extremely damp rodent in her jaws.

I stare at the animal—vole, mouse? . . . I've always been just about as good at identifying plants as at identifying vermin . . .

The *animal* thrashes about in Lizzie's jaws; kicks its paws wildly as if it's going to *annoy* Lizzie into dropping it. But, I can tell, from the look in Lizzie's eyes, that she's determined to keep the animal very much under her control.

As if to assert her authority, Lizzie gives a final—*vicious*—bite downwards.

And she puts the animal out of its suffering.

Once and for all.

With a proud few steps forwards, Lizzie deposits the animal at the toe of my rugged, mud-splattered gardening boots.

I stare down at the fragile, broken body lying in the pristine —*recently cut*—grass.

When I look back to Lizzie, I see her staring up at me, her head cocked, in the sort of expression which can only mean that she's looking for my approval.

I guess she came to the right person.

If she's looking for someone to admire killing then why wouldn't it be me?

I hear Nathan calling me again, from the back porch.

I glance down at Lizzie, then reach out my hand to her.

She rubs the side of her face—still damp with blood—against my palm.

I slowly work my hands down, beneath her belly, then lift her up into my arms; feeling the vibrations of her purrs up against my chest.

As I make my way over the lawn, headed for the back doors of the house, I chance one final glance back at the ill-fated animal; its broken body lying at all sorts of odd angles:

Unnatural, *deathly* angles.

It's only when I catch the odour of the tea brewing in the kitchen, which Nathan is about to serve me and his father; that Brian Mathewson's smiling face glimmers into being in my mind's eye.

He gives me a wink.

Then holds up his tumbler of whisky.

As if giving a toast to me.

I can't help thinking that although we went against his wishes, although I took the executive decision to stamp the Death Log into non-existence before hurling it into a particularly dirty part of the Thames; that he's—*somehow*—won.

That, in the end, we did exactly what he wanted us to.

Exactly what he *expected* us to.

But those thoughts flutter free from my brain when I see Nathan's smiling face.

When I catch sight of Mark emerging—black-and-white striped apron wrapped tight about his waist—wiping his sawdust-covered hands on the sides of his jeans.

I breathe in the now-familiar scent of sawdust; just about *everywhere*.

Because now, for the first time, it seems, I've well and truly come home.

And there's nothing Brian Mathewson—or anyone else, for that matter—can do to change it.

THE END

Author's Note

Thank you for taking the time to read one of my books. If you would like to hear about my latest releases you can sign up for my newsletter here: www.aviain.com

Thanks for reading!

AV Iain

Death Log
The Fifth Anna Harris Novel